"For goodness' sake, Edward, get up!"

The crisp, authoritative voice continued to cut through all the other noises in the room. "You've only been here a couple of hours, yet you're already molesting the chalet girls."

They both sat up. A dark figure stood in the doorway. Sarah shivered as she felt the scathing judgment of those unsmiling eyes.

"Get out of here, Edward. I can see this isn't your room." His eyes had left her. "As for you, Miss..."

"Milner. Sarah Milner, but please call me Sarah—everyone does." Sarah heard her voice sounding level and composed and felt better. After all, despite appearances, she'd done nothing wrong—while he had hardly shown the best of manners. His scrutiny of her had been so close, she was sure every inch of her figure was engraved on his mind.

"I can see you favor the informal approach with your guests."

Carol Gregor is married with two children and works as a journalist. She lists her hobbies as "reading, first and foremost, followed by eating and drinking with friends, gardening and films. I am also a private pilot, but a lapsed one since becoming a mother!"

Books by Carol Gregor

HARLEQUIN ROMANCE
2732—LORD OF THE AIR

HARLEQUIN PRESENTS
1074—MARRY IN HASTE
1129—THE TRUSTING HEART

When Winter Ends

Carol Gregor

Harlequin Books

TORONTO • NEW YORK • LONDON
AMSTERDAM • PARIS • SYDNEY • HAMBURG
STOCKHOLM • ATHENS • TOKYO • MILAN

Original hardcover edition published in 1989
by Mills & Boon Limited

ISBN 0-373-17043-2

Harlequin Romance first edition August 1989

CHAPTER ONE

'OH, NO!'

She had only turned away for a second, but in that time the onions and garlic which should have been sweating gently in the bottom of the casserole had transformed themselves into a smoking black mass.

A string of mild but emphatic epithets in both English and French accompanied her desperate attempts to limit the damage, but it was a hopeless task. Nothing in the pan was remotely edible any more.

Still cursing under her breath, she scraped the remains into the bin, ran water on to the pan and threw open the window to let the hissing steam escape.

Outside, the sky was a brilliant blue, the snowy mountains glittered with a brightness that hurt the eyes. For a second she stood transfixed, wishing passionately that she was up there on the slopes, the fresh snow spraying away from her skis as she cut a swooping path down the mountain.

Up there she felt free and strong, whereas in this steamy, unfamiliar kitchen she felt only a rising sense of panic.

She mopped her forehead with the arm of her sweater and wondered how on earth she could provide dinner for six in less than five hours, when the shops were shut and she had ruined the essential ingredients for the beef carbonnade with which she had planned to welcome the hungry new arrivals.

Then she began to bang the pans angrily in the sink.

'Yuk! What a horrible smell.'

She turned. Framed in the doorway was a young man, curly-haired and grinning. His careless smile only aggravated her stretched nerves.

'It's burnt onions,' she snapped. 'What do you want?'

'Chalet girls don't burn onions. They're all cordon bleu graduates who've earned their colours turning out executive lunches for merchant bankers and advertising executives. Everyone knows that.'

'Well, this one does. She burns anything she can lay her hands on—chicken, potatoes, pastry. You name it, she burns it! What's more, her crêpes are as tough as old boots and her soufflés sink like stones.' She began to rummage in the fridge for emergency supplies. 'Now, what do you want? Because I'm in the middle of a crisis and I haven't got time for idle chit-chat.'

'I found the door open downstairs, so I didn't bother to ring the bell, I just came in. But perhaps it's a good job I did. I can probably help with your emergency.'

'Help?' Her face slowly transformed with joy. 'Oh—you're from the store! Of course, you've brought my vegetable order! I wasn't expecting it until tomorrow.'

The man was clearly English, but there were plenty of young foreigners working at menial jobs in the village simply for the joy of spending the whole winter on the French ski slopes.

'Have you got the onions and the garlic? Because

if you have, I've just about got enough time to start again. It's really important, you see. There's a new party arriving tonight, and they absolutely mustn't find out their chalet girl's a complete incompetent in the kitchen.'

His grin widened. 'I'm not from the store—but I can cook. Let me see.' He levered himself off the doorframe and inspected the contents of the fridge, methodically laying out a small array of provisions on the table. 'Have you got any cumin?'

She shrugged. 'I don't even know where the spices are kept yet. I only got here yesterday. Annabel—the chalet girl here—was carted off to hospital with appendicitis earlier in the week. I'm her emergency replacement. A girl from another chalet has been holding the fort, but she hasn't done a very good job. The whole place was in the most terrible mess. It's taken me hours to clear up and change the beds. I've only just started to think about food.'

As she spoke, the young man was opening cupboards and drawers, making himself at home. 'Aha! Cumin.' He sniffed the packet. 'A bit old, but it will do if I roast it. That brings the flavour out. How about chicken in yoghurt with cumin and lemon, with rice spiced with peppers and tomatoes?'

Even as he spoke, he was donning an apron and flourishing a knife. She shook her head, too relieved to care who he was or what he was doing there. He was probably a friend of Annabel's, she decided, although certainly not a boyfriend. Annabel made no bones about her preference for older men, with mature bank balances, while this young man looked little more than a teenager, with the slight and wiry body of a boy.

Yet in the kitchen he was entirely in control and

she jumped obediently to his detailed orders of how to prepare the peppers and skin the tomatoes.

She made him coffee while the chicken simmered gently in its pot.

'What are you going to do about befores?' he asked her. 'And afters? If you can ruin a simple stew, I'd hate to see your fruit flans.'

'One of the chalet girls from down in the village stopped by and left me a lemon meringue pie, and I found some pâté in the freezer, so there's no problem. I can just about manage toast—if I concentrate!'

She smiled at him, her earlier panic slowly receding. Whoever he was, she was infinitely grateful to him. He had a pleasant face, she decided, albeit a little youthful and unformed. He, in turn, looked at her over his coffee-mug, taking in the vibrant vigour of her healthy slimness and lightly tanned face.

Her hair was a natural streaked blonde and her eyes were blue and alive. She wore a white shirt, the collar turned up, under a baggy turquoise sweatshirt, and black leggings that showed off her perfect figure.

'What's your name? No, let me guess. Umm— Caroline or Susannah or Victoria—shortened to Tory, of course, by close friends.'

'Sarah, actually.'

'Sarah. Actually.' He mimicked her vowels. 'Well, near enough. And I bet the family estate's in Wiltshire or Oxfordshire. Or maybe it's a town house in Chelsea or Knightsbridge.'

'It's a farm. In Bedfordshire.' Her voice grew cooler.

'A Bedfordshire farm. Well, that's appropriate enough, I suppose, provided the acreage runs to four figures. And I dare say there's a suitable young Nigel or Charles waiting at home for you to get your youthful wanderlust out of of your system so you can settle down to breeding the next generation of gentlemen farmers.'

She did not bother to contradict him. His teasing was tiresome, and if she had not felt so grateful to him he would have begun to irritate her greatly.

'I know all about it,' he offered conversationally. 'It's the same for me. Not a Nigel or a Charles, of course. But an awfully nice girl called Amanda. The only thing I can't understand——' he wagged a knife at her as he prepared to lift the chicken from its pot '—is why you can't cook. It's the only piece of the jigsaw that doesn't fit.'

'I can't cook because I've never had time to learn. I've been too busy——'

'But that's how chalet girls get their jobs. By offering up their cookery certificates.'

'I'm not a chalet——' She bit back her protest. She wasn't a chalet girl, but from now on she had to act the part to the very best of her abilities. Starting now. 'I've got other talents.'

He leered cheerfully. 'I can see that. But the ski companies usually demand a bit more than nice eyes and good legs.'

'They've got it,' she snapped.

'Oh?' He lifted an eyebrow.

'I've got a degree in French and German, and a business studies diploma,' she rapped out truthfully.

He recoiled in horror, half mock, half real. 'My God, an intellectual!'

'I'm also an expert skier,' she pressed on, 'and terrific at personnel problems. I've got the stamina to stay up half the night and still be on duty before breakfast, and I've got a stomach strong enough to cope with the all too many guests who find themselves somewhat tired and emotional after a night on the town. That's why NewSki took me on.'

'They were prepared to overlook your burnt offerings for the breadth and depth of your other skills?'

'Yes. They were.'

Of course, it hadn't been quite like that. Her cooking skills, or lack of them, had never been an issue when she had taken up her management job with the company, and it was only an unhappy set of circumstances that had led to her being here at all.

Most of her time was spent in the London head office, coping with anything and everything that came her way, as the tiny company burgeoned into a major winter sports travel company.

From time to time she flew out to Italy or Austria, to sort out a management crisis on the spot, and she managed to snatch enough flying weekends to the Alps to keep her winter tan topped up and her skiing muscles in shape.

But she had always known she was temperamentally unsuited to the life of a chalet girl, and it was only extreme loyalty to Brian and Gail, NewSki's young owners, that had led her to this French chalet, to don the uncomfortable mantle of general cook and dogsbody for the forthcoming fortnight.

She sighed. Already it was proving far more difficult than she had anticipated. But she owed them a lot. She wouldn't let them down if she could possibly help it.

'And no one's found you out? Not all season?'

Her concentration jerked back to the young man, his bright blue eyes on hers.

'Er—no, not all season. They've always been having too good a time to care very much.' She took refuge in evasion. 'I've mostly been in the bigger chalets where you get the younger groups who are more interested in skiing and drinking and getting off with each other than in haute cuisine.' It was almost true. Those were the kind of chalets that usually had a spare bed for her flying visits.

'It won't be like that here. This chalet's by far the most expensive in the brochure.'

' "A luxurious, traditional hide-away for those who like to ski in style and elegance",' she quoted, and pulled an apprehensive face. 'It's a wonderful place, have you seen the main room? It's got sofas that just swallow you up and a huge open hearth. And the balcony's divine. It looks right down the valley and it must get the sun all day. I went out there just now and I could have sunbathed in a bikini, it was such a sun-trap. Even my room is fabulous, although chalet girls usually have to double up with the hot-water boiler in the basement.'

'So why aren't you ecstatic at your sudden elevation?'

She grinned inside a little at the inappropriate word, but at the same time there was a fist of fear in her stomach.

NewSki's chalet girls knew her as one of their bosses. Yet for the first time she was realising that in many ways their job was much harder than hers, and she wasn't at all sure she was up to it—let alone the extra high demands of this particular job.

'I'm on my own here,' she confessed. 'The chalet only sleeps six guests, so there's only one chalet girl—and a lady who comes in every morning to help clean. I won't have anyone to help me out with the food. And I have a nasty suspicion that the people on their way here are not exactly happy-go-lucky types. I've got strict instructions to ladle on the charm for a Mr Holloway, whoever he is. I get the impression he's already been hassling them about this and that and warning them that he expects the highest standards in everything——' She cupped her hands round her coffee-mug and stared out at the mountains. It had been more than that.

'Pull out all the stops, Sarah,' Gail had instructed her vehemently. 'He's not an easy man to deal with, but he's an important client—probably the most important NewSki will ever have. I can't tell you any more, not at the moment. I'm sorry to be so mysterious, but as soon as I can tell you, I will. Meanwhile you must understand—it's vital that nothing goes wrong, nothing at all.'

'I wish Annabel was here,' she said forlornly. 'She's one of the company's best girls. She would have known just how to handle him——'

The man was arranging neatly cut chicken portions on a plate. 'Suppose I told you I'm Mr Holloway?' he said casually.

'You?'

Her blue eyes slid from the mountains to the figure in blue jeans and a white Aran sweater, curly hair growing waywardly over his collar. Horror and incredulity fought within her.

If he was the dreaded ogre, then her nervous chatterings were an utter catastrophe, and yet—— Surely he couldn't be the man who had forked out thousands for this luxury chalet? He had no style, absolutely no aura of power. It was impossible to imagine him setting the capable Brain and Gail on their ears.

'I don't believe you.'

'I am. Edward Holloway. Commonly known as Ned.'

She felt the colour drain from her face under its tan. She swallowed. 'Are you serious? I assumed you were a friend of Annabel's. You've really booked this place for a fortnight?'

He came towards her, brandishing a lemon, and peered at the look of apprehension on her face. Then he laughed, not a pleasant laugh but the chuckle of a spoiled boy who likes pulling wings from flies.

'You look terrified! Don't worry, I won't get you the sack—provided you're nice to me. I won't even tell them who made the supper.'

He turned back to his work, whistling under his breath. She was too stunned to move from the stool where she was perched.

'Actually,' he said at last, 'I must confess I'm not *the* Mr Holloway. The Mr Holloway——' his voice twisted a little as he spoke '—is my big brother, James. And I can well imagine him putting your bosses in a stew. He demands the best and he gets it. And if he doesn't . . .' His voice tailed away as he shook his head in a telling fashion.

'Oh.' She watched him wordlessly. 'Are you one of the group?'

'Yup.' He flashed her a look. 'A co-opted member. Drafted in at the last minute to make up numbers. I must confess I wasn't looking forward to it very much, skiing's never been my forte, but I can see now I'm going to enjoy myself a lot.' His eyes went over her until she felt she had to move. She began to wash pots. 'I'm here early because I came down from Paris. Everyone else is flying in from London.'

'What were you doing in Paris?'

He paused while his eyes mocked her. 'Cooking, I'm on a year's secondment in a hotel there. In fact, maybe we could come to an arrangement.' He paused, speculatively. 'I'll do your cooking, if you do my—er——' his eyes slid over her '—skiing!'

'There's nothing I'd rather do——' All her instincts told her to have nothing to do with his offer, but the words were out before she could stop them. She didn't want to be in his debt, but in tight corners you had to use whatever resources were to hand. Even so, she drew back.

'I'd love some help, but at what price?' she probed, lightly. 'Because you ought to understand I'm not in the business of paying for favours in kind.'

He smiled broadly at her, although his eyes held a shadow of cunning. 'This holiday isn't going to be a lot of fun for me, Sarah,' he confessed with a rueful grin. 'You'll see why when you meet my elder brother. One of his favourite pastimes is giving me a hard time. I never quite come up to the standard of relentless perfection in everything that he demands. I would be quite glad of the chance to escape to the kitchen and remind myself I have some useful talents.'

'Oh.' She softened, realising he shared her apprehension of the days ahead, and chose to ignore the calculating light in his eyes in favour of his endearing, youthful smile. 'Then I must confess I'd be only too grateful for any sort of tips or help you could give me. And if it could be kept quiet from the other guests, I'd be even more grateful.'

'A secret. Ooh, I love secrets! In fact——' he poured sauce with expert skill over the chicken '—I'll tell you a little secret. Yours isn't the only one I'm keeping.'

'What do you mean?'

'Aha.' He tapped the side of his nose. 'I can't tell you—it's a secret!'

He really was tiresome, she decided, but she would be quite willing to put up with a measure of irritation if he helped her over the hurdle of providing breakfast and dinner for six hungry skiers every day, not to mention the cakes and buns they would need for tea.

'Will you?'

'Help you? Yes.'

She felt relief untense her shoulders. She guessed full well that his help in the kitchen might lead him to expect other favours in return, but, she decided, she would cross that bridge when she came to it. Surely, with all her management skills and experience, she would have no trouble turning aside any unwelcome advances from a young man like this?

'Thank you, Edward.'

'Ned.'

'Ned, you're a pal. I'll just get the pâté out, and I'll show you your room.'

'You haven't put me in with James, have you? I warn you, I'll leave right now if you have. It's bad enough having to put up with him all day, without having him at night as well.'

She turned to him, frowning. 'Is he really that bad? You make him sound like Attila the Hun.'

'He is to me. If it's not one thing, it's another. The bedroom is one area of my life I've managed to keep to myself so far, and I don't want to be told my pyjamas are the wrong colour and the window needs to be open. I can just hear him now, boring on about the virtues of fitness and fresh air.'

She thought fast. 'Well, you're not in with him.

I presume you're one of the two singles, so you're in the room off the living-room.'

The other single room was right next to hers, the two rooms shared a small bathroom, but she didn't want this leering young man as close to her as that. 'Who's the other single?'

'Big Brother. He was coming with his girlfriend, but that seems to have come to a rather abrupt end, so yours truly was drafted in to make up the numbers. I don't suppose that will have improved his temper,' he added philosphically.

'I see.' She frowned. In trying to distance herself from young Ned Hollway, it seemed she'd lumbered herself with the dreaded older member of the family. Well, she'd only got herself to blame, and anyway that put James Holloway as far as possible from the upstairs kitchen, while Ned would be on hand for urgent culinary queries.

'I don't know who the others are,' he volunteered. 'James and I keep our distance. All I know it that one's an American called Brad and he's with his wife whose name I've forgotten, and the others are called Tim and Kerry. Tom and Jerry, I call them.'

She laughed, despite herself, but the apprehension she had felt earlier, and which Ned's unexpected arrival had partly dispelled, began to gather again. All her instincts told her that this did not sound like a happy party of friends, and that the two weeks ahead were likely to provide a minefield of difficulties.

She sighed and looked away out to where the sun was sinking in a rosy haze behind the peaks. The fading light made the pine trees that framed the window dark and forbidding, and as she looked one or two lights went on in the village down the hill.

Well, she'd had a wonderful two years with NewSki, loving every minute of her demanding job and the opportunities it had given her for skiiing in any number of different resorts. And there had been the added satisfaction of seeing the company leap from strength to strength.

But at twenty-four she'd already learned the simple truth that everything had to be paid for. And if the price of her great good fortune was now to be two weeks of pretence, and menial labour for prickly clients, then it was a price she was quite prepared to pay.

'*Voilà*!'

The chicken lay on a large oval platter, garnished with fine curls of lemon rind and toasted almonds. It looked superb. Everything else was set out by the cooker, ready for last-minute preparations.

'Ned, it looks lovely. You're a genius.'

'I know. Now I think I deserve a bath, a sleep and a stiff drink before the rest of the troops arrive. What time are they coming?'

'About six. I think. That's the time the coaches usually get here from Geneva. They drop people off all the way up the hill. Since we're the highest chalet, we're probably last port of call. It could be seven, or even later.'

'The later the better, I say.'

She showed Ned his room, looking quickly round to make sure the quilt was properly plumped and the towels on the rail were carefully folded. She watched as he dumped an obviously expensive case on the bed.

'Ned, what does your brother do?'

He seemed to grow deliberately vague. 'James? Oh, he's in business.'

'What kind?' she pressed him.

'Um—I'm not really sure. Sports and leisure. That sort of thing. You know. The new leisure society.'

'I see.' She didn't, really. She found it hard to reconcile the picture she had of this saturnine ogre with a manufacturer of squash rackets or jogging suits, and she felt sure Ned was being deliberately evasive. Probably the man was a crook, she thought savagely, a bent accountant or a cocaine importer. Well, it didn't matter to her. Just as long as he stayed out of her hair.

'I'm going to crash,' Ned announced, falling on to the bed. 'Wake me at six, will you? Preferably with vodka and tonic. Heavy on the vodka and easy on the tonic.'

Even as she watched he shut his eyes, and, stifling a desire to tell him to do his own fetching and carrying, she shut the door.

With dinner all but ready, she had a chance to tidy round the kitchen and make final preparations. She checked there was ice in the freezer and logs in the log basket. She lit the fire and watched smoke begin to curl up through the sweet-scented wood. She drew the red velvet curtains across the balcony doors, set the table and fanned out magazines and newspapers on the coffee-table.

The room looked warm and welcoming, exactly the thing for tired and chilled travellers.

It was half-past five, just time for a bath and a change before she had to wake Ned—a thought which made her heart sink a little. The chalet was so quiet and peaceful now, it was almost like being alone.

She went to her own room, unzipped the case which she had not yet unpacked, and took out a vivid blue jersey sheath dress, frowning at the crumpled garment.

She hung it up in the steam of the bathroom while water splashed into the old-fashioned tub and went to unpack her small stereo set and put on her favourite tape of the moment—highlights of Verdi's *Otello*.

The music and the hot water soothed her jittery nerves, restoring her customary confidence. She wrapped a towel around her and carried the music, still playing, back to her room.

For once she took time to pin her hair into a high knot on her head, and tease tendrils around her face. She put on her make-up and stood up to dress.

As she did so there were suddenly fingers holding her bare shoulders.

'Oh!' she cried out in shock.

The soaring music had masked the sounds of Ned coming in through the carelessly open door, and his touch had scared her half to death.

'What do you think you're doing?'

She turned savagely, instinctively fighting him off, and as she did so she tripped on her case which lay still open on the floor, and went sprawling across the bed, taking Ned with her, his weight landing on top of her with a shock that took her breath away.

'Mmm—this is a more enthusiastic greeting than I'd expected——' His arms pinned her to the bed as his lips playfully sought hers.

'Ned——' She twisted away from him in protest, feeling as she did so her towel unwrap itself. Her legs flailed uselessly under his body, and her careful hairstyle came adrift, but the struggle was in vain. She felt his lips home in on the soft skin of her neck and shuddered.

'For goodness' sake, Edward, get up! You've only

been here a couple of hours, yet you're already molesting the chalet girls! I despair of you!'

A crisp, authoritative voice cut through all the other noises in the room.

They both shot up.

A dark figure stood in the doorway. Sarah took in an impression of height, black hair, and a cutting look.

She shivered as she felt the scathing judgement of those unsmiling eyes, and she realised as she did so that she was towel-less and completely naked.

Too shocked to blush or move, she froze. The man looked at her coldly, but closely, making her feel like a laboratory specimen on a slide until Ned slithered off the bed on to his feet.

'Brother James,' he drawled as he took his time about getting up. 'As untimely as ever.'

His voice broke the spell. She knelt up, searching hurriedly for her towel, but it was not on the bed. Ned had pulled it to the floor as he got up. Stranded, with no cover to hand, she did the only thing she could think of doing. With all the dignity she could muster she swung her legs off the bed, stood up, bent to pick up her towel and quickly swathed it around her. As she anchored it firmly beneath her arms she managed to look coolly in the direction of the doorway.

'Get out of here, Edward. I can see this isn't your room.' His eyes had not left her. 'As for you, Miss——'

'Milner. Sarah Milner. But please call me Sarah, everyone does.' As she spoke, and heard her voice sounding level and composed, she began to feel better. After all, despite all appearances to the contrary, she had done nothing wrong. While he had hardly shown the best of manners. His scrutiny of her had been so close, she was sure that every inch of her figure was engraved on his mind.

'I can see you favour the informal approach with your guests.'

There was sarcasm in his tone. She focused on his face and saw a disconcertingly penetrating gaze, from unusual eyes that were so dark a blue they were almost navy. 'I hope you're not as casual about your other duties——'

'What happened was an accident, wasn't it, Ned?' she said levelly.

She looked round and found to her annoyance he had already slipped away. She looked back to his brother. 'Edward startled me—I didn't hear him come in. I jumped up and we both fell over my case. Look——' She pointed to where the buckle of the case had grazed her ankle. 'I can imagine how it must have seemed from outside, but it wasn't like that at all.'

'And just what was Edward doing in your room in the first place?'

'I've really no idea,' she said with annoyance. He's your brother, she was about to add, but just in time she remembered her newly humble position, and the two difficult weeks that lay ahead. The most important clients NewSki had ever had, Gail had warned her.

'I suppose he needed something and came to look for me. I was just getting ready to greet you all.'

'So I see.' The dark eyes went swiftly over her bare shoulders, the white towel and slim legs beneath it. 'Well, perhaps you could hurry up, so we could all be given our rooms.'

'I'm sorry I wasn't ready. You're earlier than

expected. I thought the coach would drop you here last.'

'We didn't come on the coach, I hired a car to bring us from the airport. I didn't much fancy being cooped up with a load of drunken hooligans singing rugby songs for four hours.'

Her lips quirked a little. It was an all-too-accurate description of some of the tour groups, she knew, but most people were prepared to take such high spirits in good part, especially when they were about to start a two-week holiday.

'I see.' She looked at him coolly for a moment, then turned on one of her most professional smiles, radiant and impersonal, one she had often used to good effect when dealing with disgruntled clients. 'Well, if you'll give me one moment of privacy, I'll be with you. Perhaps you could leave your bags in the hall and go upstairs for a drink. Everything is set out ready.'

And even as he took in her look she advanced towards the door and closed it firmly in his face.

CHAPTER TWO

AFTERWARDS she stood and shook for a full two minutes, quailing at what lay ahead. She had expected James Holloway to be difficult, but she had developed a mental picture of him as a silver-haired executive with gold-rimmed glasses and a remote manner. The man who had surveyed her naked figure so closely could only be in his early thirties, and had an overwhelming presence. And difficult was an understatement for the cold and critical look she had seen in his eyes.

More than that she could not say, because she had not let her eyes focus too closely on him for fear of losing what little composure she had managed to gather around her.

But once she left her room and began settling everyone in their rooms there was no more time to think, although none of the new arrivals lifted her spirits. Besides the slippery Ned and the glowering James, there were four others, and not one of them exuded the high-spirited *joie de vivre* she had seen in other chalet parties.

Brad was an American, polite enough but quiet, with a nervous, twittery wife called Barbara. Tim and Kerry were a younger couple. Tim was lanky and loud, with a drawling voice and a laugh that shook the rafters but seemed curiously lacking in humour, while Kerry's elegant beauty was marred by a sulky mouth that spoke of boredom and petulance.

No one seemed to know each other, and, although James had introduced everyone with impeccable social ease, even his heart didn't seem to be in it.

Well, they'd just have to get on with it, she thought savagely, as she cut and buttered the toast and fanned it out on to hot plates. Didn't they know they were in some of the finest skiing country in the world? Right in the middle of it, in fact, so that from their own front door they could ski down to the main lifts and from there go for miles and miles and miles without once retracing their steps.

And didn't they know that this chalet was one of the finest in the area, snug and luxurious under its snow-laden eaves? And that the snow this year was the best that France had seen for decades? And that the restaurants were first class, and the nightlife reputedly lively, and if only they let their hair down a little they could have the holiday of their lives?

Well, she'd tell them all that, but it was up to them if they chose to enjoy it or not. You could take a horse to water but you couldn't make it drink—although drinking seemed to be one thing they did relish, she thought, remembering the size of the second gins that Brad had dished out all round.

On the whole, she thought, it was probably a good job she wasn't a master chef, since any fine cuisine would be ruined by such pre-prandial excesses. Athough if they carried on as they'd started it might be her very salvation, since none of them would ever be in a fit state to notice the quality of the food set before them.

None, except James Holloway, she thought sourly, whose glass had stayed empty the second time around and whose dark eyes seemed to miss little as they surveyed his guests.

She'd watched him covertly from the kitchen and been able to take in more carefully this man that had put the London office of NewSki into such turmoil.

He was, by any objective standard, extremely good-looking—far more so than she had realised at first. His hair was thick and almost black, although in the lamplight there were faint auburn lights in its depths, his features were strong and his profile was even. He was tall, with broad shoulders, but he wore his size lightly, moving easily about the room.

But it was his eyes that were so arresting. When she had first seen him she had thought they were dark blue, but now they seemed much lighter, more grey. She stared more closely, unable to help herself, fascinated. Their darkness came from a darker rim of navy around the iris, and from the clearness of the whites, which caught the flickering firelight as they ranged over his gathered guests.

He was one of the most handsome men she had ever seen, she decided, but his looks left her as unmoved as a shop-window model would. She looked at his mouth. His lips could have been chiselled from stone because there was a tightness about them that spoke of a chilling lack of warmth. In fact, his whole face seemed closed and clenched like a fist, and the only expression she could read there was the bored politeness of a dutiful host.

Idly she wondered what his thoughts were, because whatever they were they were obviously giving him little pleasure; as if reading her mind, James flicked up his eyes and looked directly at her, his gaze enigmatic on her own blue, intent stare.

And as he looked at her she knew without a shadow of a doubt that he was stripping away her blue dress and seeing again the high firmness of her small breasts and the curve of her narrow waist and slender hips, and after that he seemed to look deeper, right into her mind, and the tangle of hostile thoughts that seethed there.

She blushed a little now, remembering the uncomfortable jolt of that look, and at how edgy he made her. She felt he could unmask her as easily as he was now peeling cellophane away from a new packet of cigarettes for Kerry, and that notion made her very uncomfortable indeed.

She waited until she had regained her normal composure, then went out. 'We can eat if you're ready.'

The fire was crackling nicely, and the table looked cheerful with its red candles and sparkling glasses. She looked to James. 'Would you like to organise the seating? I'll take the end seat, near the kitchen.'

When she returned with the pâté she saw he had taken the seat at the head of the table, next to her. Ned was opposite.

She made sure everyone helped themselves, then, since conversation seemed to be flagging, she offered to tell them about the resort.

'Oh, God, spare us the purple prose,' Kerry drawled. 'We can all read, after all. Why don't we just ask you things when we need to know them?'

She blanched, taken aback by the unexpected rudeness, and looked automatically to James. He met her look and she knew, although she could not have said how, that he was angry at the girl's response, but schooling himself not to show it.

Ned said, 'This is delicious pâté, Sarah.'

She flicked her gaze to him. 'Annabel made it and put it in the freezer—before she was taken ill.' She looked to James. 'The chalet girl here was taken to hospital earlier this week with appendicitis. I was drafted in at rather short notice, I'm afraid. I think I've found my way round by now, but if I seem hesitant about anything in the chalet, that's the reason.'

'I see.' He frowned. 'I trust you at least know the resort.'

'Yes. Yes, I do.' She met his look as levelly as she could. It was not exactly a lie. She had had several holidays here. But if James had any idea at all about who she was, and how she came to be sitting here, he would probably be on the telephone to London straight away with a barrage of complaints.

She remembered how the telephone had rung in the office three days ago, and Gail, taking the call that told her of Annabel's medical emergency, had gone white.

'Oh, my God, I don't believe it. Poor girl—but why did it have to happen this week?' she had cried, putting the receiver down. Sarah had run to fetch her a glass of water and made her sit down.

'Couldn't we draft in a girl from one of the other chalets?'

'No. None of them is good enough, and anyway they're all needed where there are.' Without going into details, Gail had made it clear that this was a chalet party that had to have the very best of everything. 'If I was in a fit state, I'd go out there myself, but——' She had indicated the mound of her stomach.

'They wouldn't let you on the plane,' Sarah had said crisply. 'Not at eight months pregnant. And quite right, too.' And, accepting that, Gail had looked up with sudden speculative look in her eye which had caused Sarah to burst out, 'Oh, no, not me, Gail, I'd be hopeless—you know I've always said I could never bear to be a chalet girl—I can't cook, and I hate being given orders——'

But somehow, despite her repeated protests, Gail had won her round. Persuasive businesswoman that she was, she had made Sarah feel that she, and she alone, could solve the crisis. She had praised her skills of diplomacy and management, told her she looked like a million dollars, made light of her lack of culinary skills, and played heavily on their friendship.

And it was that that had been the winning card, Sarah reflected. Gail and Brian had taken her on directly from college and given her every chance to grow in her job. She owed them more than a few favours in return.

Added to which, Gail's pregnancy had been difficult, and twice it had seemed she might lose the baby. The last thing she wanted was for her to have extra stress and worry at this late stage. She frowned deeply.

'I hardly think it was that difficult a question— unless you are having to make up an answer.'

James' voice, hard, cut through her thoughts. She looked up and found him scrutinising her expression.

'I'm sorry——'

'I said, how long have you been here? All season?'

'I've known it for years,' she parried, and quickly glanced round the table. 'Please do ask me if you need any help with anything, and if you want me to come along and translate, I speak fluent French. I notice you haven't all got your own skis and boots, for instance. I could show you the best place to hire them from.'

She risked a glance back at James, and saw with a tremor of apprehension that her evasion had not escaped his notice. He looked sceptical and displeased. But Brad saved the moment, saying, 'Perhaps you could take Barbara under your wing. She's never been skiing before. She's always refused to learn in the States, but now she's in Europe she's decided to take the plunge. She needs gear, lessons, the lot.'

'Of course.' She stacked plates busily and brought the chicken from the kitchen.

'My,' said Ned as he tasted it, 'this is wonderful. Cumin, isn't it? You must tell me how you get it to taste so fresh.'

His eyes mocked her. She gave him a vicious look. 'I roast it,' she said curtly, wishing she could roast him. 'It brings out the flavour.'

'Well, that *is* a handy tip,' said Ned, with enthusiasm so obviously faked that she was sure the others must see it. 'I must say I look forward to your other meals. You're obviously a first-class cook.'

'Praise indeed,' said James drily. 'The one thing Edward does know about is cooking.'

'My brother is so kind.'

She looked round. This was awful. Usually on the first night everyone would be talking skiing, recounting old adventures and wanting to know about local conditions, but this was like a stiff and prickly dinner party that refused to get off the ground.

'Will you be making an early start tomorrow? The snow's fantastic. It snowed all yesterday and the ratracs have been busy all day smoothing the runs.'

'I never make early starts,' Kerry drawled. 'It's a policy decision I took long ago.'

Brad said, 'You bet. Tim and I thought we'd tackle the Jean Blanc.'

'That's the trickiest black run in the area,' she said, frowning. 'It's hard for even the most experienced skiers. But I suppose you know that. Although someone told me yesterday that the ice is really bad on the top at the moment. There's a narrow gully where there's barely room to turn, and that has turned into an absolute glacier. You just can't get a grip with your skies.' She looked at James as she spoke and was glad to hear her voice sounding confident and authoritative.

Yesterday she had flown around the resort like a demented hen, piecing together as much local information as she could gather from the other chalet girls, the ski instructors and a few old friends she had winkled out.

Brad said equably, 'Sounds like fun. What do you say, Tim?'

Tim's eyes were glazed from drink. 'Sure, it'll do for starters. We'll get a bit of practice on that and then go off piste——'

'If that's what you're interested in, you can hire a guide at the ski school.'

'To hell with guides——'

She looked anxiously to Brad, who said, 'That's just the wine talking. We'll get a guide. Don't worry, Sarah, I know the dangers. Skiing's practically my living. And Tim tells me he's pretty nifty on skis.'

'Are you, Tim? Have you done a lot of skiing?' There was an edge in her voice, and she saw James shift in his chair at her side. Maybe chalet girls shouldn't challenge their guests like that, but from all her experience with NewSki she guessed Tim might be just the type to over-reach himself and come a cropper.

'Enough. Perhaps you could pass down that

bottle.'

She handed it silently down to him, her eyes glinting like ice in the glacier she had just spoken of.

'Where have you skied?' she persisted.

'Oh, here and there. Italy. Austria,' He met her assessing eyes. 'What is this—a bloody inquisition? I haven't come here to be interrogated by the servants.'

How dared he? She flushed angrily and jumped up at once, throwing down her napkin on the table. It knocked over James' glass and sent a stain of wine across the table before she quickly righted it.

Noisily she began to stack the plates before biting words fell from her tongue. It was Ned who broke the awkward silence.

'I don't think you can exactly call Sarah a servant. Why, she's got a degree in modern languages and a diploma in business administration. Isn't that right, Sarah?'

She turned away to the kitchen unable to trust her voice, but acutely aware that James had half turned in surprise at Ned's words to watch her retreating figure, slim and supple in its sheath of blue jersey. She could feel the glare of his anger, like a headlamp, on her back.

She served the lemon meringue pie in silence and left them to themselves, retiring to the kitchen to wash plates and make coffee.

It was ironic, she thought as she slowly calmed down, that in London she avoided such domesticity like the plague. Her busy job usually left her so exhausted at night that she either ate out, with friends, or in, alone, from a takeaway carton. Yet the rhythmic, mindless chore was surprisingly enjoyable and she was quite lost in her own thoughts when a noise startled her.

James stood in the doorway, his face hollowed with shadows and tiredness.

'I'm turning in early tonight. I wanted to thank you for the meal. It was excellent. If you keep up this standard for the fortnight there will be no complaints at all.'

She fought to control the guilty flush of colour that rose to her cheeks, and after a difficult second or two she succeeded. 'Thank you. I'll certainly try.'

He paused. 'However,' he continued and there was a crack of ice in his voice, 'I found your abrupt departure from the dining table a quite unnecessary show of pique. It made my guests feel most uncomfortable.'

'*They* felt uncomfortable?'

He ignored her, saying what he had come to say. 'I realise Tim's remarks were not in the best of taste, but as an experienced chalet girl, you must know only too well how people's tongues get loosened after a few glasses of wine.' She was rooted to the spot. Was it her imagination, or had there been an ironic emphasis on those words 'experienced chalet girl'? Had she been found out so early? She was so busy thinking about that, that it took a second or two for the full weight of his remarks to sink in. When they did she had to struggle to master herself before she was able to reply coolly.

'I'm sorry if I upset anyone. I felt that, as a *servant*,' she laid sarcastic emphasis on the word, 'I was probably better off in the kitchen, getting on with the chores.'

'Well, in future please stay at the table until dinner is finished. I would not like any of my guests to think you were trying to avoid them.'

'Very well.' You're the boss, she added with mental insolence.

But so, too, under normal circumstances, was she, and she had a sudden piercing longing to be able to confront James Holloway on her own ground and to let him see her for what she really was.

She looked at him with barely masked hostility. His eyes were on hers, darkening as he looked at her, and he showed no sign of moving.

'I hope you sleep well,' she said pointedly. 'The hot-water pipes are a little noisy in those downstairs rooms, but it stops once the tank has filled up.'

He nodded, understanding he was being dismissed. 'I could sleep on Waterloo Station tonight with no trouble,' he said, almost civilly. 'Goodnight.'

'Goodnight.'

She stood staring at the empty doorway, quivering with anger and confusion. How dared he tell her off like that? His comments had struck deeply at her pride. And yet there had been a weariness in his face which had been at odds with the harshness of his voice.

He must have chosen to come here, chosen his guests, but he had the air of someone who wished profoundly he was somewhere else, in other company. Although maybe it was simply tiredness——

'Aha!' Ned swooped into the kitchen and grabbed her by the wrist. 'This holiday is looking up! I love a bit of aggro.'

'Stop it.' She disentangled his hands, covering the movement with feigned laughter. 'They loved your meal.'

'Didn't they just, though! Tomorrow night I thought you'd cook stuffed tenderloin of pork, and the day after roast veal——'

'Hold on. I've got a budget to keep to! And, Ned——'

'What?'

'I don't see how it's possible, anyway. You'll be out skiing all day. You won't have time to help me.'

He pulled a face. 'Not if I can help it. Nasty cold stuff, snow. And those hideously uncomfortable boots—— No, I've got it all worked out. Kerry seems to be my sort of girl. Her idea of a day's skiing is a long, slow breakfast at a café in the village, followed by lunch on the mountain somewhere, a short, gentle descent down a beginners's run, to a couple of brandies at the bottom, and then home for tea. And since Big Brother has positively instructed me to keep her company, I'll have plenty of free time.'

'He's "instructed" you?' she repeated, incredulous.

'Well, it's his party.' Ned's voice was defensive.

'For a party, it doesn't seem to be affording him much fun. He's gone to bed already.'

'Ah, well, you know what they say, all work and no play—— James has been practically killing himself over the past year to put together some sort of American deal. That's what this little gathering is all about, I understand. A kind of thank you to all those who were instrumental in bringing it to pass.'

'You mean, they're all just business acquaintances?'

He flapped his hands. 'For heaven's sake, don't ask me details. I'm just a humble trainee chef. The world of high finance is quite over my head.'

She sighed, and turned to lean against the sink, crossing her arms. 'Business entertaining! What a way to ruin a chalet party. Roll on Wednesday, I say.'

'What's that?'

'My day off.'

'Oh, ho!' Ned advanced, his hands reaching for her waist again. She pushed him away.

'Don't get any ideas. I'll be up at dawn and at the top of the mountains before anyone here has even surfaced. And you won't see me again until long past dark.'

'And then?'

'Then I'll have a long and leisurely bath and go off to visit friends. Off duty is strictly off duty. Company rules.' She should know, it was she who had revised the agreement on time off when one or two girls had complained that clients were making unwanted claims on their free time.

'In that case, I'll have to sqaunder my attention on Kerry. I don't get the feeling she's that enamoured of Tim, do you?'

She shrugged. 'I'm only the servant, remember? It's not my place to have opinions about the guests. Now, if you'll excuse me, I'm off to bed. I'll have to be up stirring the porridge at seven o'clock.'

'Think you'll be able to manage?'

'If I try hard. And if not, I'll come banging on your door.'

'Please——' He put up a hand. 'Like Kerry, I don't have early starts. When it comes to breakfast, you're on your own! But I'll leave you some instructions for supper.'

'Surreptitiously, of course?' She was anxious, more anxious than before. Now that she had finally met James Holloway, she really didn't fancy his reaction if he found out she was so completely

incompetent she had had to co-opt one of his guests
as chief chef.

'Of course—but all this has a price, dear Sarah.'

She tipped her chin. 'What's that?'

'I haven't quite decided—just let's say I'll expect
you to be as nice to me as I'm being to you——'

She favoured him with one of her widest client
smiles, white teeth and sparkling eyes, but inside she
sighed wearily, foreseeing tedious scenes ahead. Not
that Ned Holloway held any real fears for her—unlike his elder brother whom, she felt sure, could
wither her any time he chose with a look or a well-
chosen word.

But Ned was scared of James, too, she thought, as
she made her way downstairs, and that was a great
advantage, since he would be quite unlikely to risk
creeping downstairs to rattle her doorhandle in the
middle of the night, and her spirits rose at the
thought that she would soon be snuggled down under
her duvet, with no need to encounter any one of this
awkward bunch again until morning.

'Oh!'

The bathroom door opened unexpectedly as she
went past, and she cannoned headlong into James as
he emerged from the warm and steamy interior.

His hand shot out to steady her as she stumbled.

'I'm sorry,' he said.

She was so close to him as he righted her that the
warm smell of his body enveloped her totally. She
saw a powerful chest, sprinkled with dark hair, a
towel stretched tautly about his hips, and felt his
hand, strong and sure, on her arm.

She looked up, startled by the sudden assault on her
senses, and saw a completely different man from the
forbidding presence that had graced the dinner-table.

His hair was tousled, softening the hardness of his face, and his eyes had lost their coldness and were a warm, deep blue. His face had been white with tiredness, but was now damp and flushed.

They were flung together by the surprise impact and their glances seemed to lock with the same abrupt force. It was as if they were seeing each other properly for the very first time, she thought, and she suddenly stepped back, breaking the hold of his hand, because in that quick moment something strange and disturbing had happened deep inside her, and she did not like it one bit.

'It's my fault. I wasn't looking where I was going.' Her voice sounded odd, thin and shaky. 'I —hope you sleep well.'

His eyes went over her face, too slowly for comfort.

'Goodnight, Sarah.' Like his gaze, his voice had warmed and slowed from his previous crisp harshness. There was a sensual quality in it that had not been there before and it made her swallow.

'Goodnight.'

She went hurriedly on into her room, but could not stop herself turning for a quick backward glance as she opened the door. James' door was already closing. Once he had looked his fill he had obviously not felt any need to turn back to her.

Then she sat down on the bed, holding herself hard by the elbows, trembling from what had so abruptly happened to her. The warm, almost sharp smell of his flesh was still in her nostrils, and the power of the look they had shared seemed burnt on her brain.

When he had held her arm she had wanted to put out her own arms and pull him to her, and when she had seen the look in his eyes she had wanted to throw back her head and offer her lips up for him to kiss her.

It had been abrupt, animal instinct, as powerful as any primitive urge, and coming as it had, out of the blue, it had thrown her completely off balance. Now the pulses of her body were throbbing and hammering as the blood drummed through her veins, roused and urgent. She took a shuddering breath, trying to calm herself.

This was the last thing, the very last thing in the world she would have wished, or wanted. She was going to need all her wits about her if she was to steer her way unscathed through the next two weeks, and, if there was any one thing she did not need to complicate the picture further, it was an unrequited crush on the cold captain of this unstable crew.

CHAPTER THREE

IT WAS a wonderful morning. All her customary cheerfulness flooded back to her as she shopped in the village, enjoying using her French again and feeling the sun warm her face.

You could tell winter was beginning to recede by the strengh in its rays, she thought. In a few weeks' time the mantle of snow would begin to melt and spring flowers would start to push up on the mountain pastures.

Usually that would mean a slackening of the pace in NewSki's office, but the company had grown so fast it now had operations in every part of the world, and there was never a time when the work eased off completely.

She was proud of the key role she had had in this. By persuading Brian and Gail to open a second small office right in the City of London, and by overseeing a carefully targeted advertising campaign, she had helped NewSki get a healthy slice of the new Yuppie market. Young brokers and bankers poured through their doors, willing to pay thousands of pounds for a chance to ski in North America, or Australia.

But she had been working a twelve-hour day for most of the year and she was tired of the relentless pressure, just how much so she realised when she paused on the steep road back up to the chalet to catch her breath and stood watching the skiers coming down the runs on the opposite side of the valley.

They moved like colourful dots on the snow, swinging this way and that, while the cabins of the main lifts rose out of the main terminal area in a constant stream, taking new loads of skiers up to the mountaintops.

It was quiet enough to hear water dripping from the icicles of a nearby chalet roof, and the crisp mountain air set her sluggish city blood tingling.

She smiled, suddenly delighted to be here. The problems back in the chalet weren't that bad, she told herself in a new burst of optimism. Ned would help her out with the cooking, and as for James—well, with great effort, she had scarcely thought of him all morning.

He had not appeared at breakfast, and he had obviously gone out because when she got back she found the chalet was as silent as a tomb.

'Whew!' She put down the bags with relief. Ned's shopping list, left with the cooking instructions he had promised her, had been extensive. It was a good job she was a hundred per cent fit or she would have had trouble getting back up the hill with that load.

She unzipped her padded jerkin, and hoofed off her moon boots. If she worked fast she'd have time to do most of the basic preparations before fulfilling her promise to meet Barbara in town and take her off to the ski school.

On bare feet she carted her load upstairs and began to put things away in the kitchen. The sun streamed in and her work made her hot. She stripped off her jersey and worked in her T-shirt and tight leggings.

There was a cassette player on the window ledge which must have been Annabel's. She switched it on and rock music pulsed out, its beat matching her raised spirits. She danced across the kitchen, opened

an unfamiliar cupboard door, and suddenly found
baking trays and dishes crashing in an avalanche of
metal around her feet.

'What the hell is all this noise?'

James stood in the doorway—black trousers,
black sweater, black mood, she noted among her
confusion. Another baking tray slid noisily on to the
floor.

'I didn't think there was anyone here.'

She turned and fielded another falling tin, then
risked a second look back at him. Her pulses were
hammering hard, but it was impossible to tell
whether it was from the shock of his presence, or at
the noise of the toppling kitchenware.

But it was all right, he didn't have at all the same
effect on her as he had had last night. The angry,
controlled man who stood before her, hostile eyes on
hers, left her quite cold.

She turned fully to face him, flooded with relief
that she had not turned helpless victim to an inexplicable teenage infatuation.

'So I gather from this wretched adolescent pop
music!'

'It isn't pop music, it's rock. The Rolling Stones.
You can't call them adolescent. More geriatric.' Her
indifference to his physical presence gave her new
confidence. He ignored her.

'It's impossible to work with all this racket going
on.' His eyes swept over her form.

'Work?' Her eyes registered surprise.

'Yes, work,' he snapped. 'Most people have to.'

'I assumed you were out skiing.'

'I don't ski.'

She looked at him, her lips opening in surprise,
then she frowned, trying to take in what he said. He

might as well have spoken in Latvian or Serbo Croat for all the sense his words made to her.

'You don't ski,' she repeated slowly.

His face was set.

'That's what I said. Do you have a hearing problem? I don't ski.' The words were hard and icy, then he swore suddenly and violently under his breath, and strode across the kitchen to snap the pounding tape off.

Her eyes followed him, and when he turned back to face her she saw a dark anger in his face which was out of all proportion to her astonished repetition of his statement.

Yet she still could not take in the fact that someone could come here, to this place, this chalet, and not want to ski.

'If you wanted to learn, I could easily arrange lessons for you. There's a wonderful instructor here, Claude Montaine, who speaks perfect English.' He was an old friend of Brain and Gail's, and she had got to know him well during his visits to London. 'And it's an ideal place for beginners. All the runs near the village are easy ones, green or blue.'

She stepped forward, fired with evangelical fervour, her hands out to emphasise her words. 'It's the most marvellous sensation ever! You really ought to try it. And I'm sure you'd be a natural.' Last night, seeing his close-packed muscles, the litheness of his movements, she'd assumed he was an expert skier. 'Let me book you a day's trial.'

'No, thank you. I'm sure you mean well, but I'm here to work and that's all.' His voice had been cold and controlled, but it suddenly harshened. 'I don't want trial lessons with Claude Montaine or any other Tom, Dick or Harry of the ski slopes. All I want is to be left alone to get on with things—in peace and quiet.'

Her hands dropped as if felled by the force of his anger.

'I'm sorry. I just thought——'

'Well, don't. You're not paid to think! You're paid to run the chalet and look after your guests. On present form I'd say you were only managing to fulfil the first half of your duties. If you care at all about the good name of your company, I suggest you start to try a bit harder with the second!'

'Oh! How dare you? That's so unfair——' She automatically began to protest against the gratuitous insult, then bit back her words, remembering her loyalty to Brian and Gail. Silently she began to pick up the fallen pans until she had gained control of herself.

'This was an accident. It won't happen again.' There was a frosty dignity in her voice.

'Make sure it doesn't,' he said curtly, and walked out.

She stopped and stared at the empty doorway, mouthing the rudest word she could think of into the space he had left behind. It hardly helped.

But at least, she thought later when her outrage began to cool, his revelation had quite killed off any lingering echoes of last night's inexplicable surge of longing.

There was no way, no way at all, she could ever contemplate getting involved with someone who did not share the overwhelming joy and passion of her life, and if James Holloway had no urge to know what it was like to come winging down the mountain with the wind in his face and sparkling whiteness all around, then he was a total mystery to her—and one she had no desire to unravel.

She worked quietly, relieved to find Ned's instructions detailed and precise. He had assumed she was a culinary imbecile and had left absolutely nothing out, which was quite correct, but she began to realise that under tuition like this cooking could easily cease to be the mystical rite she had assumed, and become a skill like any other, easily mastered with practice.

When she had finished she whisked through the rooms, making beds and straightening curtains. James' room gave nothing away about himself. The case by the bed was expensive, the book on the side-table the political thriller that everyone was reading this season. It was almost as if he did not want to be here, and had done nothing to make himself feel as if he was staying.

She paused outside the main room, wary of disturbing him, but her hesitation was only brief. After all, she thought fiercely, she had her work to do, just as he had his.

The door was half-open and she saw him ensconced on the sofa, papers spread about, long legs stretched out, a briefcase computer open on his lap. His concentration seemed total, yet he said without looking up, 'You can come in.'

'I was just going to. I have to tidy up and clear the fire.' Her eyes flashed to his bent head. 'I'll be very quiet,' she added with sarcastic emphasis.

She began to work immediately, stacking books on the windowledge and plumping cushions. As she knelt to sweep the ashes from the grate she sensed his eyes stray to her figure. Well, let him look, she thought savagely. Her rear view was one of her best features, kept slim and trim by constant exercise—

and she could hardly be blamed if he allowed himself to be distracted by it.

But then the very devil seemed to seize her, and she brushed out every nook and cranny of the fireplace, twisting and wiggling provocatively, until every last speck of soot had been thoroughly dealt with.

As she rose, James was frankly watching her and their glances snagged together with disturbing complicity. 'An admirable performance,' he said drily.

'I don't know what you mean. I was just doing my job.'

'A remarkably thorough job.'

'I hardly think you can complain about that.' She nodded at his papers. 'I'm sure you like to work in the same way.'

'I do. But who said anything about complaining?'

'Perhaps it's simply what I've come to expect——'

'You mean I've found fault with everything so far?' He pushed his computer away a little, looking up with an expression that still held an echo of dry amusement.

She pushed back her hair. 'It's your right to, if you feel things aren't being done properly.'

'Quite,' he said, crisply, and reached for his computer again. 'However, I can hardly complain, now, about the cleanliness of the fireplace, can I? And I'm sure you'd like to know that the shapely rear end of the chalet girl also meets with my full approval.' He held her eyes with a coolly taunting look and she suddenly blushed with shame at the childish game she had permitted herself.

As she left the room she paused, looking for a way to make amends. 'I have to go out now, to help Barbara. You do know the chalet doesn't provide lunch, don't you?'

He nodded, apparently absorbed in his work again.

'There's some ham and cheese in the fridge, but if you go out, L'Interlude is the best place in town for light meals.' She hesitated. Outside the sun shone brilliantly, but it would not get round to these windows until after lunch. His figure in the gloomy room looked grim and austere, almost lonely. 'Is there anything I can get you?'

'I'm fine.' He looked up briefly and coldly. 'As I thought I made clear earlier—the only thing I want is peace and quiet.'

Three hours later she had reason to reflect that she could do with some of the same, since Barbara twittered and clung to her throughout the laborious business of kitting her out with boots and skis. She shrieked when she tried to walk in the unfamiliar footware and complained that the skis hurt her shoulder when she carried them. The first time she tried to stand on her skis, on the snow, she squealed like a stuck pig.

And when Sarah explained that, having delivered her safely to the ski school, she intended to leave her in the capable hands of the class instructor, her face went stiff with terror.

'Go on.' She pushed her firmly in the direction of the group of beginners. 'Think what you'll have to tell Brad tonight when you get back.' Barbara's face was white, but once the woman saw there was no alternative she set off doggedly across the snow.

Sarah left without a backward glance, running to the *pâtisserie* before all its best cakes were sold. Normally chalet girls whipped up their own scones and sponges, ready for the hungry skiers when they returned at dusk, but she knew her limitations. Providing a passable dinner was going to tax her quite enough.

Luckily a day's skiing seemed to relax everyone a little. From where she worked in the kitchen, the conversation around the tea-table sounded easy enough, although when Brad came in for more hot water she realised new tensions were emerging in the difficult group.

'How was it?'

'Great. But Tim——' He shook his head. 'He's really wild. He takes everything too fast. He doesn't respect the mountain. I've said I'll go out with him again tomorrow, but after that I'm going on my own.'

Next it was Barbara, wrapped in a robe and gulping a brandy.

'I'm never going back there!' she moaned.' It was awful. Everyone kept laughing at me when I fell over. Even that dreadful little man, Pierre.'

'Pierre laughs at everything all the time. You're lucky, he's said to be one of the better instructors.'

'I can't understand a word he ways. Isn't there anyone who speaks better English?'

'Well, there's Claude Montaine—but he only takes a few selected pupils. He owns the ski school, and he's a racer. Instructing's just a hobby of his.' And he wouldn't touch you with a barge-pole, she added silently to herself. She turned back pointedly to the soup she was stirring, and after a moment or two Barbara departed. But her peace was short-lived.

'Got you!' Arms clamped round her waist.

'Get off, Ned,' she said, without turning from the cooker.

He ignored her. 'Did you follow my instructions?'

he breathed into her ear.

'Stop it, you're tickling. Yes, I did. Look.' She pointed to the fillet lying ready to be roasted. Ned eyed it without letting her go.

'That looks fine. Ten out of ten. Now for my consultation fee.'

'Your what?' She tried to laugh him off, turning to face him and attempting to break his grip on her waist.

'My fee. We're going to the disco at Les Halles tonight. I want you to come, too.'

Her heart sank. She had been told about the place—told it was over-decorated, over-priced, and patronised mainly by the over-forties.

'Oh, Ned, please.' She put her hands up to his chest to push him, away.

'We need some more tonic out here.' James strode into the kitchen, cast a glance at them and opened the fridge door. 'Since you seem to be far too pre-occupied to attend to the needs of your clients, Sarah, I'll get it myself.'

'Big Brother seems somewhat dyspeptic,' Ned observed, slowly letting her go. 'Have you worked all day, James? You should have got some mountain air. It's wonderful for clearing away the cobwebs.'

'Since when have you been even remotely interested in what I do with my days?' James snapped. 'Or fresh air, come to that. But since you ask, yes I have been working. And now I'm getting Barbara and Kerry a drink—a small courtesy which you could have attended to, if you hadn't been otherwise engaged.'

Ned turned to her and pulled a conspiratorially rude face. She struggled not to respond but a smothered, nervous giggle escaped her. James scythed her with an evil look, and she felt a whole new sympathy for Ned, forever on the receiving end of such contempt.

Ned reached over and took the bottle from him, swung a folded tea towel over his arm like a waiter and swayed insolently out.

She glanced angrily at James, but he got in first.

'I don't know what NewSki's policy is towards chalet girls getting involved with their clients, but I warn you now, I don't want any embarrassment to my guests.'

'I can tell you exactly what the company's policy is!' She should know, she had helped to draft it. 'It employs people for certain hours, to do certain things. It doesn't own them body and soul. What people do in their own free time—and with whom—is entirely up to them, provided it does not bring the company into ill repute.'

'I hardly call this your free time.'

'And I hardly call a friendly—and entirely uninvited —embrace, an involvement. By that token most chalet girls would be clocking up half a dozen affairs a day.'

'Whatever it was, or wasn't, my guests' needs were not being seen to.'

She turned and faced him squarely. 'If you had asked me, I would have willingly brought more tonic. As it was, when I set out the drinks table this morning there were two large bottles of tonic on it. That's usually more than enough to last all day——'

'If you're implying——'

'I'm not implying anything.' Her voice was crisp with anger. 'I'm simply stating the facts. Since you seem to want to do everything in your power to imply I'm not up to my job, you can hardly blame me if I choose to marshal the case for my defence.'

She challenged him with a look, her habitual air of
authority shining clearly through her casual chalet
girl camouflage, and he was forced to acknowledge
what she said with a slight nod of acceptance. She
watched him look away, then, as if he did not know
what to make of her, and as he did so something
changed in his look that sparked a betraying wriggle
of excitement deep inside her. It was as if he had
looked at her, really looked at her, not just her body
but the person she was inside it, for the first time, and
his eyes told her that in spite of himself he liked what
he was finally seeing there.

'Right,' Ned declared later, coming back from the
telephone. 'A table for seven at Les Halles, and a taxi
to take us down the hill.'

'Seven?' Tim raised an eyebrow.

'Sarah's coming, too.'

'Is that usual? I mean, do chalet girls normally
socialise with their clients? Shouldn't you be
whipping up a chocolate soufflé for tomorrow night
or something?'

He laughed his humourless guffaw, but Sarah
could see he meant every word of it. He clearly saw
her as a service for which he had paid, and now
expected his money's worth.

As did James, or rather as had James. Throughout
dinner he had been curiously attentive to everything
she said, and when their eyes chanced to meet she
was sure he was seeing her in a new light.

She bridled. 'It's profiteroles, actually. And
they're already in the fridge.' She did not add that
she had bought them that afternoon at the *pâtisserie*.
'As to whether chalet girls socialise with their guests,'
she looked pointedly at James as she spoke and was

amazed to see his mouth crook with hidden humour, 'well, it depends on the guests. Both sides can be rather fussy about these matters!'

She looked all round the table. Ned was enjoying himself. Tim looked taken aback, like a stuffed fish. Kerry and Brad and Barbara were talking among themselves and had missed the exchange, but James—her eyes stopped when they finally went back to his because in them was a clear look of appreciation and a warmth that went right to the innermost parts of her.

She took a breath and her mouth went dry. Her heart was thumping. When he looked like that, when his face unclenched from its harshness, then he did things to her that no one had done for years.

No, she corrected herself silently. Not for years. Not ever before. And she felt suddenly frightened and way out of her depth.

The last time she had let herself get involved with a man, she had ended up so badly hurt that she had vowed it would never happen again. Work and more work had flooded in to fill the howling emptiness that was left after his departure.

But even in the first, heady days of that affair she had never felt quite so excited and frightened as she did when she met James Holloway's unmasked navy gaze.

CHAPTER FOUR

AFTER her exchange with Tim Sarah had no choice but to go along with Ned's arrangements. Her plan to make a public plea of tiredness and retire to her room had been thwarted by his arrogant challenge.

She dressed to meet the challenge, knowing she looked good in a white cashmere shift which ended a fashionable few inches above the knee and showed off all her youthful slimness.

She made up carefully, so that dark eye-make-up highlighted her eyes, and her lips were outlined in clear pink, and she teamed that pink with matching tights, belt and hair combs which pinned her hair away from her fine cheekbones. She packed high-heeled shoes into a bag to change into from the boots she would need to wear to and from the taxi.

She told herself she was doing it to put Tim in his place, but she knew it was all really for James, although what she felt about him she did not dare examine too closely.

He was rude, arrogant, humourless—the list of his vices endless. She did not like him, or anything he stood for. But that one unfathomable glance tonight had thrown all rational thought out of the window.

'Wow!' Ned whistled vulgarly when he saw her, and claimed her to sit on his knee in the crowded taxi. James got in next to them, taking in her appearance with one swift burning glance, and she was acutely conscious of her leg touching his as they drove down the winding road to the centre of the resort.

As the car drove cautiously along the icy roads, they passed a small doorway with a discreet sign outside, and she turned her head, wishing the taxi would stop at that door.

She knew that that unpretentious cellar bar was the gathering point for all the really serious skiers in the area, and she would have loved to spend an hour or so talking shop with the instructors, the ski guides and travel agents who had made it their local.

As she looked she saw the familiar figure of Claude Montaine shouldering his way through the door, head bent against the cold. She turned, looking out of the back window at him, and as she did so she saw James, too, look round sharply.

It was most peculiar. If she hadn't known for certain he was a non-skier she would have sworn he recognised either the dim-lit doorway, or Claude's muffled figure.

She looked directly at him in puzzlement, her lips opening to frame a question, but to her astonishment he glared furiously at her before looking abruptly away.

It was all over in seconds and no one else in the cramped taxi had noticed anything, but she was certain she had not imagined it, and the curious incident occupied her mind for the rest of the drive.

Les Halles was as ghastly as she had been warned. They sat in an alcove lined with red plush and watched the dancers on the mirrored floor. Sarah quickly drank the champagne that Tim had ordered and sipped at another glass. Although not normally a drinker, she knew it would irritate Tim to see how much of the expensive bottle she was consuming. More than that, though, was the need to muffle the restless fire that James had sparked within her.

Even as they sat at the table, every fibre of her being strained towards where he was in conversation with Kerry, occasionally removing his eyes from her low-cut cleavage to cast dark glances across at her.

Brad asked her to dance. 'I can't believe I'm here,' he told her, steering her around the floor. 'I've only been to Europe once before. Colorado's my usual stamping ground.'

'Is that where you live?'

'That's right. I own a chain of sports shops all along the mountains. Least, I *did*. I guess James owns them now. He bought me out about a month ago. Now I just get to manage them, and James has all the real headaches. Built them up from scratch,' he added.

'Don't you mind—selling them?'

He laughed. 'When James has his eye on something you might as well throw in the towel there and then. He never takes no for an answer. I said no over and over again——' He looked down at her mildly. 'I did mind a bit. It was like seeing a baby grow up and leave home. I guess that's why James invited me along on this trip—sugar on the pill.'

She laughed. 'I'm afraid Barbara doesn't see it that way. She had a tough time in ski school today.'

'Oh, Barbara, she likes to flap and fuss about things, but she's tougher than she looks. She always said she didn't want to ski, but now she's changed her mind she'll stick it out. She'll settle down in the chalet, too, after a few days. New people aways make her nervous.'

'I know just how she feels.' She pulled a face, then reverted to the topic that occupied all her thoughts. 'James told me he doesn't ski—I could hardly believe it.'

'I know. It's incredible, when he's in the sports business. He plays good tennis and a mean game of squash, but he just doesn't seem interested in learning—he doesn't even want to discuss it. Quite gave me the cold shoulder when I offered him the chance to learn.'

It was reassuring to know she was not the only one, she thought, and her eyes strayed to the table where James lounged back to his seat, his dark gaze on her. Her heart jolted as she met his eyes.

The music faded down and became low and slow, and she saw him stir, and she was certain he was about to come and claim her from Brad. She even shivered in anticipation, but then she saw him throw himself back in his seat again as Ned swept her up into his arms, in a stifling embrace.

She tried to wriggle loose, but he only gathered her closer, his hands roaming down her back to the swell of her buttocks.

'Ned, stop it!' she hissed, her eyes on James, but his face had become a hard, shadowed mask.

'Stop what?'

'That.'

'You owe me a few favours, Sarah. You seem to forget.' Ned had been drinking heavily, and his voice was slurred and menacing.

'If it means this, you can forget it. I'll manage without your help.'

'Brother James won't be very pleased with burnt offerings.'

'Brother James can lump it. Some of the other girls will help me out, if I ask them.'

'NewSki are pretty keen to keep old James sweet,' he said pointedly.

'I know that.' That was, after all, exactly why she

was here. Athough she had not been very effective in her task so far.

'But do you know just how sweet?'

She shook her head.

'I'm supposed to be keeping it a secret. God knows why. Business etiquette, I suppose. But I can tell you something—you need yours truly far more than you think you do.' He paused dramatically, staring down at her. 'They want to sell. James has said he might be interested—but only if the whole company's in good running order. And that means the highest standard all round. That's why he got the best chalet——'

Her eyes opened wide, 'And he would have got the best chalet girl—if only Annabel hadn't fallen ill!'

Her thoughts turned rapidly. No wonder Gail had been so keen to keep him happy. She and Brian had always made it clear to her that they would want to sell the company once it grew beyond a certain size, and this past year they had been actively looking for buyers.

The two of them had long wanted to start a small, exclusive ski school in one of the Swiss resorts, so they could settle down among the mountains they loved so much, but they had begun to despair of ever finding anyone who wanted to take NewSki on.

Brian had said despondently, 'All the big operators already have their own outfits, and there doesn't seem to be anyone around who wants to get a foothold in this business.' And Gail had added, with feeling, 'Can you blame them? It's hardly the easiest way to make money. You have to be mad about skiing—or just plain mad—to do this for a living.'

Her thoughts churned. Of course, she should have realised just what it was that made James so special, but the rush to get out here, and then the struggle to cope, had left her little time to wonder what it was all about.

Ned's arms tightened round her, but she was oblivious of him, or her surroundings.

Selling the company now would be the best thing that could happen to Gail, she thought. If a deal went through she could relax and look forward to the birth of her baby with peace of mind. It was her duty to do everything possible to ensure the deal went through, but her record as a chalet girl so far was hardly exemplary.

She sighed. From now on she would have to try harder, accepting James' harsh criticism meekly, and putting up with Ned's advances in order to secure the help she so sorely needed in the kitchen.

'What's the matter?' Ned crowed. 'Don't you fancy James as your boss?'

'Oh, shut up,' she muttered, but so softly he hardly heard as he bent to nuzzle at her neck. Thankfully at that moment the music faded and she was able to excuse herself and head for the cloakroom.

Outside, she bumped headlong into Claude Montaine.

'Sarah, *ma chère*!' He kissed her warmly on both cheeks. 'What are you doing 'ere?' Playing chalet girl, they tell me,'

'Just for a couple of weeks. Annabel was taken ill, and it—it seemed a good chance to get some grass-roots experience. But don't tell anyone, will you? I'm supposed to be the genuine article.'

He shrugged. 'OK. My lips are gummed.'

'Sealed. Anyway, what about you? I saw you going into the Skiers' Bar earlier. This isn't your sort of place.

He pulled a face, his mobile features expressing rueful necessity. 'A very rich client, with royal connections! I managed to get out of giving her lessons by passing her over to Victor, but this is the price I have to pay. Being seen with her at this whorehouse!'

'Claude, it isn't!'

'I know. I know. But all that red velvet——' He shuddered.

'I'm on duty, too, with my chalet party. Honestly, Claude, they really are a bunch. Do you know there's only one decent skier among them? The others either can't ski, or don't particularly want to. Can you believe it? Coming to nightspots like this seems to be their idea of a good time—and I don't even think they're enjoying themselves now. I must go, they're expecting me back. Bye.'

She kissed him warmly, wishing she could invite him to their table. But when she saw him later he was in the very farthest corner of the room, in a dim alcove whose intimate gloom was only occasionally pierced by the sparkling lights of his companion's jewels.

Some time later, though, he passed nearer to hand, as he guided his guest through the tight-packed dancers, and he lifted a sympathetic eyebrow to her before his gaze swept over the group at her table.

As he did so his face seemed to stiffen with surprise. She saw him stop, freeze, and look back over his shoulder, before the music compelled him on into the throng. She stared after him, trying to see if he would look back again, but by then the room was thick with cigar smoke and it was hard to see anything clearly.

She shook her head to clear it. Maybe she was imagining things. She certainly felt about as edgy and unrelaxed as it was possible to be.

Brad had taken Barbara on to the floor. Ned was dancing with Kerry and Tim's eyes were on them as they giggled together.

She felt uncomfortable sitting between Tim and James, and sipped again at her glass. Her head was pounding and she wanted more than anything in the world to go home to her bed.

'I suppose you want to dance,' Tim drawled, ungraciously, and began to rise to his feet.

Immediately James sprang up and held out his hand to her. 'I was just going to ask Sarah if she would dance with me. Please, I'd be glad if you would.'

She went on to the floor with her heart knocking, but then he turned her expertly into his arms and she went with surprising ease into his firm embrace.

At once she was aware of his body, lithe and poised, and the way she seemed to fit into his arms as if she had been made to do so. It was the first time they had deliberately touched, and she was sure he was every bit as aware of it as she was. For a few moments they moved slowly together, not speaking, and a powerful tide of desire seemed to rise up and enclose them in a private world of wanting.

Her body was throbbing, urging her to move closer to him, and she knew that he was equally roused, but instead of pulling her nearer he deliberately moved back, setting her a little apart from him.

And when he looked down at her, his cynical expression denied their physical intimacy.

'You have quite a talent for this kind of dancing.'

'What do you mean?'

'I was watching you with Ned.'

'Oh.' She did not know what to say. How could

she possibly explain the web of deceit that she was trapped in?

The new closeness that she had sensed between them earlier in the evening seemed to have evaporated into the smoky air and she felt desolate without it. So desolate that it was surprisingly easy to say meekly, 'I'm sorry if you think I shouldn't have joined the group tonight. I know it annoyed Tim, but it was difficult to refuse when Ned had already made the booking.'

'I thought you wanted to.'

'Oh, I did.' But not because of Ned, she willed him to understand, because of you.

'I see.'

No, you don't, she thought, you don't see anything. Not who I am, or why I have to put up with your beastly brother. She felt tired and sad, and longed to rest her forehead on his broad shoulder and unburden herself of all her troubles. Instead she said stiffly, 'It was nice of you to rescue me from Tim. But it doesn't bother me—his attitude.'

'The man's insufferable,' he bit out.

She looked up, surprised. In the gloom his face was only angular planes and his eyes were darkness.

'I'm sure he doesn't mean to sound as he does.'

'I only wish that were true. Sarah——' she sought his eyes as he used her name '—I realise that this isn't the easiest of chalet parties for you to look after——' Suddenly he broke off, and whatever he was going to say was forgotten as his eyes strayed from hers to the scene over her shoulder, the corner where Claude was sitting.

For a moment he froze, and then with casual purpose he steered her back into the thickest throng of dancers, turning his face from that part of the room. Other couples closed in on them, pressing them together, and after a few moments, as if by mutual consent, they yielded up to the pressure.

Their closeness swept everything else from her mind, as the music seemed to hold them in a world out of time, and she could feel the length of him, thighs, stomach, chest, against her. They stood swaying, barely moving, not speaking, enveloped in their private closeness, until James settled her more firmly still in his arms, spreading his hands on her back to hold her tenderly.

Without thinking she lowered her head and rested it on his shoulder. It felt so good, she wanted to stay like that for ever. Slowly, as the effect of the drink and the myriad tensions of the long day finally took their toll, her eyes fluttered closed and dimly she felt James' hands move up from her waist to her shoulders, and then to the soft skin of her neck, to cradle her head against him.

'Psst!'

Her eyes flew open. Ned and Kerry were going past them. Ned's eyes awash with alcohol. Over Kerry's shoulder he raised his eyebrows in mocking surprise at them, then blew her an elaborate kiss. She drew back, embarrassed, and James, who had turned and caught the gesture, suddenly broke his hold of her and led her back to the table.

Tim said, 'I've ordered another bottle.'

James' voice was curt, almost angry. 'Not for me, thanks, I'm going to turn in.'

'The taxi's not coming for another half-hour.'

'It doesn't matter. I'll walk. I'd like the air.' He nodded at Tim, then Sarah. 'Goodnight. Enjoy the rest of your evening.' His look was dark, black, impersonal. What had just happened between them, the tenderness they had shared, might have all been in her imagination for all he showed of it, she thought miserably.

Then he was gone, leaving her and Tim alone at the table in the thickening smoke.

She sat tense for a moment or two, then she jumped up. 'Please excuse me Tim.' She would not, could not, spend another moment there, not another second.

She flew out of the door, waited restlessly while the cloakroom attendant hunted for her coat and the pair of boots she'd brought, then sped out into the night.

It was glorious out, crisp and clear. Ahead, in the deserted street, James strode out, a dark figure in his black parka.

She had been about to hasten after him, but there was something about his solitary figure, a stroke of darkness against the whiteness of the silent snow, that made her falter.

Abruptly the thought came to her out of nowhere that he was a figure in exile, deeply alone and removed from everything that warmed and informed the person he was. And somehow she knew she was right, and that buried deep in that thought was the key to the mystery of a man who seemed so harsh and joyless, yet whose eyes, when he let them, told her a quite different story.

She stood in the empty street, arrested in her tracks and as she watched he grew more distant, the gap between them widening with every step he took.

'Wait, wait for me!' She could not bear to lose him.

He stopped, turned in surprise, then waited for her to catch up. The air was so cold, it rasped in her throat as she hurried towards him.

'What do you want, Sarah?' His voice was as frosty as the glittering banks of snow around them.

'Oh!'

She recoiled from its crackling harshness, suddenly seeing how her uninvited appearance must seem to him. In her headlong rush to leave the disco she had not stopped to consider his feelings.

She shook her head urgently, embarrassed.

'Look, I know what you're thinking, but you're wrong. I'm not pursuing you, or anything like that. I'm not after you—please don't think that. I just had to get out of that place. I'd really had enough. I thought I could walk back with you.'

'Why don't you wait for Ned?' His voice was still harsh, his eyes hostile.

'Ned's busy.' She was short. She did not want her name linked with Ned's in any way.

'I see,' he said, but he turned and began to walk on, more slowly, as if assuming she would fall in step with him. 'With Kerry? Is that why you had to get out?'

'No!' She stopped and glared at him, entreating him to understand. 'No,' she repeated more calmly. 'It's just that I doubt if he or any of the others will want to leave till closing time. While I've got to be up at seven, making breakfast.'

'It's a hard life, being a chalet girl.'

Was he mocking her? She glanced at him, but his face was as impenetrable as usual.

'It can be—when things go wrong.'

'What like?'

'Oh, burst water pipes, stolen ski gear. People falling ill.'

'What about people falling out?'

'What do you mean?'

'Chalet parties can be explosive things—people thrown together for weeks at a time, late nights, too much to drink——'

'Most people get on fine. Even when there are tensions, they make an effort to overcome them. They're on holiday and they want to have a good time. I've never known a party that didn't enjoy itself.'

'Until now, you mean.'

She was surprised at his candour.

'It's early days,' she said cautiously.

He swore lightly. 'Early days be damned. I warn you, the only way this unholy crew can go is downhill.'

She walked in silence beside him, taking in his bitter words, the only sound the snow as it squeaked and crunched under their boots.

'Brad's nice, and there might be more to Barbara than there seems.'

'Yes,' he conceded. 'Although I can't say she's my kind of woman. As for Tim—the man's a barbarian. If he carries on the way he's started, I'll be hard put to it not to punch him on the nose before the two weeks are up!'

She laughed out loud, amazed at his openness. 'Ned told me they were business acquaintances of yours, not friends.'

'They're certainly not friends,' he said energetically. 'Brad's at the American end of a deal I've just sewn up. Tim's a banker, and I have to say a rather dubious one, at that. But years ago, when I was first getting started, he was the only one to stump up with a loan. I've owed him a favour ever since then. As for Ned—well, he rather speaks for himself, loud and often!'

'He's very young, still, and terribly in awe of you. I think he almost acts up to your image of him. He knows you think he's no good at anything.'

'I don't think that at all. I do think he hasn't really applied himself to anything, just lived off the family money and drifted here and there.'

'He seems keen on his chef's training.'

'Yes,' he conceded. 'It might be the thing that settles him down at last. But when you get to know Ned better—as you seem in the process of doing——' his eyes slid to hers '—you'll learn he's much better at instant enthusiasms than staying the course.'

She ignored the sarcasm. 'You're very hard on him. He's bound to kick against it.'

'Maybe. But you've only known him for a few days. I've watched him in operation for twenty-two years.'

'Are you the only two in the family? There must be quite an age gap.'

'Me being so ancient, you mean?'

'No.' She flushed. 'I meant him being so young.'

'There's a decade, and yes, we are the only two. Not that we've seen much of each other in recent years. I've been . . .' he paused, 'away a great deal.'

'Ned told me you were in the sports business. I suppose you have to travel a lot.'

James stopped dead, turning to her abruptly. 'And what else did he tell you?' His eyes scoured her face so closely, she felt he was sieving her innermost thoughts, and she felt a guilty flush stain her cheeks.

For a mad moment she was tempted to tell him everything, about his interest in NewSki and her own devious role in keeping him sweet. But then she remembered Gail's tired face, and just in time she was able to answer, 'Nothing. Why, what's the matter?'

He shook his head as if to free it from an iron grip. His face was framed by the upturned collar of his coat and there was no softness in it, only frowning lines of concentration, and a dark look under dark brows.

It made her heart beat faster, but whether it was with wanting or fear she could not be sure.

'It's all right. Let's go.'

She felt his hand taking her elbow, steering her on up the icy road. After a few moments he let her go, but whenever the going got hard he was quick to help her again. Not that she stumbled often. She was used to walking in the snow and stepped out as lithe and nimble as a gazelle beside his heavier tread.

CHAPTER FIVE

THE ICE was treacherous, however, at the steep top of the hill, and after a time James took her hand and tucked it firmly into the crook of his arm.

She almost wanted to laugh. They were like a staid elderly couple promenading to church, she thought, but, when he stopped for breath and turned to look at her, the sensuous shadowed planes of his face wiped any hint of a smile from her own features.

He looked down at her for a long moment without speaking, then looked away, into the valley below.

'What's that building there?' He pointed to a bright cluster of lights on the opposite slope.

'Where?' She stalled for time.

'Look.' He pulled her closer to him, with an encircling arm, so she could follow his line of vision.

She hesitated. 'I'm not sure.'

'I didn't even think there was a road out of town on that side. Where would it go?'

'I don't know,' she had to admit. 'Maybe just to the heliport.'

'I thought you knew the resort well?' He turned to her and there was an undertow to his question that frightened her. She thought rapidly.

'I suppose I had better come clean,' she said after a moment. 'I did mislead you the other night—but only a little. I do know the resort. I've skiied here quite a few times. But I haven't actually worked here until now. When Annabel fell ill, and there was no one on the spot to replace her, NewSki drafted me in to fill the gap.' She looked up at him. 'I worked as hard as I could before you arrived to update my knowledge of the place so I could give people the information they needed—but when it comes to outlying geography, I'm afraid I'm as ignorant as you are.'

'From where?' His eyes were scouring hers.

'Where what?'

'From where were you drafted in? Where were you working before? France? Austria? Italy?'

'No—I——' She hesitated. His eyes did not leave hers. She swallowed. 'I was free. In London.'

'In London,' he repeated. His eyes seemed to bore into her mind. 'Somehow, Sarah Milner,' he spoke very slowly and deliberately, 'I don't think you're quite what you seem.'

'And neither are you.'

The abrupt words were out before she realised she had spoken.

He caught his breath sharply. His face was so close to hers that the cloud of his breath touched her cheek and she realised with surprise that his arm was still holding her close to him.

'What do you mean?' His tone was quiet, but forbidding. She shrank from it, cursing the champagne that had loosened her lips and allowed her private thoughts to spill out in words.

'Nothing, really.' She shook her head. 'Maybe I just meant that you don't seem very happy. You don't seem to want to be here.'

Somehow she managed to meet his look, keeping her eyes open and honest. It was true. For all his wealth and power, for all his good looks, he seemed like a man with a curse laid on him.

He looked into her eyes as if he would read her

thoughts, and she looked into his and saw anger give way to something else, to a warm and hungry wanting that softened the lines of his mouth and made him move imperceptibly towards her.

She saw him move, hesitate, and sensed a short, sharp debate inside him. And she could not breathe, but stood, rigid with tension, waiting. She knew he was going to kiss her a split second before his lips came down on hers, but she did not know whether she wanted it or not.

Then she heard him mutter, tightly. 'There's nowhere else I want to be,' and his arms tightened about her. And as his cold lips took hers she knew she had never wanted anything so much in her whole life.

But there was no tenderness in their embrace, and little comfort. Her lips opened readily to his, but their mouths tasted metallic from frosty air and their skins rubbed coldly together. They struggled in vain to reach for each other against the springing insulation of their heavy-duty coats, while under their boots the snow squeaked in protest as their weight shifted restlessly.

'God dammit!' James' hands roamed her back, and went fruitlessly to the fashionable plethora of zips and buttons and ties that kept her jacket snug. Impatiently he gave up, pulling her up to him and taking her mouth harder, as if he would pour all his thwarted passion into that sole point of contact, but the kiss was an agony of frustration for them both, and she was almost glad when he dropped his arms and stood back from her, his breath rasping and his eyes burning blackly.

It shouldn't have happened, she thought with confusion. The embrace had been more a struggle than a kiss, a fight to reach out for each other, through all the many layers of deceit and misunderstanding that held them apart more effectively than the thick padding of their clothes.

'That shouldn't have happened. I didn't mean to do it.' He seemed to read her thoughts.

And I shouldn't have let you, she thought, but his harsh matter-of-factness stung a different response from her.

'Why did you, then?'

He thrust his hands into his pockets. 'The champagne, I dare say. And the night air. And the fact that you are a very, very beautiful girl.'

The compliment was stated as cold fact, and gave her no pleasure.

'And the missing girlfriend, as well?' she said tartly.

'My, Edward *has* been busy filling in all the background details.' His tone was twice as cutting as hers. 'I would love to know what else he's been telling you.' He turned and began to walk purposefully on, leaving her no option but to fall in step again behind him.

'You know, you're always down on him, but it seems to me you behave in exactly the same way! You expect the chalet girl to be on tap for your favours, just as much as he does.'

'And she is, isn't she?' He stopped and turned to her so suddenly, she collided with him and had to jump backwards. 'I didn't notice you fighting me off just then, any more than I noticed you keeping Edward at a distance on the dance-floor tonight!' His unexpected anger stoked hers higher.

'Oh!' She almost screamed with frustration. 'How many times do I have to tell you? There is nothing—

nothing, nothing, *nothing*—between me and Ned. As for tonight—you took me completely by surprise! And what am I expected to do, anyway? Put yourself in my shoes. You're the boss. My job is to keep you happy. Do you honestly expect me to push you off the side of the mountain?'

They were facing each other, both flushed and breathing hard. At her words James grinned slightly, in spite of himself.

'According to your contract you would have been within your rights to do so—as you made quite clear to me earlier.' He looked at his watch. 'I'm sure one-thirty in the morning must be "after hours".'

His eyes warmed by humour were more dangerous to her precarious emotions than any number of hostile glares. She felt her mouth go dry with wanting as she looked at him. 'Then perhaps I should have done just that!' she shouted, and marched on in angry silence.

Behind her James said quietly, 'But you didn't want to, did you?' before following her up the road.

The silence continued until they reached the chalet, and afterwards, as they took off their coats and boots in the hallway. Her heart sank as she mounted the stairs to the main room and saw the clutter of unwashed dinner things on the table.

Her head buzzed with tiredness, and James' step on the stairs behind her jangled on her stretched nerves.

'I'll give you a hand.'

'No, thank you.' Her voice was curt, and she did not turn.

'Please, Sarah. I'm not very good at apologising —but I haven't been fair to you tonight, I shouldn't have done what I did. I didn't mean to. It would be a way of making amends.'

His voice was low, warming her, but she still did not turn. Then his hand was on her shoulder, twisting her to face him. It was difficult to meet his eyes, after what had happened between them out in the frosty darkness, and when she did she found she had to look swiftly away, in case he saw how much she wanted to search their watchful depths for the man who was hidden there.

'Let me help.' It was almost a command, and she almost gave in. Then she remembered. It would hardly do for the prospective proprietor to spend the early hours of the morning helping to wash up his guests' dirty plates.

She took a grip of her jumbled emotions and said firmly, 'Thank you for the offer, but there's no need. No need to apologise, and no need to wash up. It was just something that happened.' She tried to smile, but her usual ready grin seemed stiff around the edges. 'Past history. In the morning it will seem as if it never happened.'

He looked hard at her, as if he would protest, but instead he said, 'You'll be up half the night if you tackle this lot alone.'

'I'm in practice.' The blatant lie slipped easily off her tongue. 'And anyway, I like being alone at the end of the day. It helps me collect my thoughts.'

She turned and began to clear and stack dishes, dismissing him as decisively as she knew how. Behind her James moved to the stairs, saying in a low voice. 'I'd give a few pounds to know what they are.'

In spite of herself she looked up, and he met her eyes with such an open and sensual look, so unlike his usual cold, guarded presence, that her blood was suddenly racing through her veins and her hands shook so much that she put down the plates she was holding with a violent crash.

When he had gone she worked like a woman possessed, plunging her hands into the hot suds as if she would scrub and rinse the confusions from her mind.

How could she feel like this about a man as cold and hard as James? A calculating businessman whose life seemed to afford him no relaxation, and even less pleasure? Oh, she understood the pleasures of working hard, but that, for her, could never be enough. There had to be other things—friends, music and above all skiing.

She paused in her work, thinking. James spurned skiing, her greatest passion, and chose instead to spend his days shut away from the sparkling mountain scenery in a gloomy room, with a briefcase full of papers. How could she possibly be attracted to a man like that?

She pulled a face and attacked a blackened frying pan. Of course, there was a perfectly simple explanation.

James Holloway, with his tall figure and dark hair and strong face, was an incredibly handsome man. His lips were straight, his eyes compulsive, his voice deep and strong. And not only that. There was an aura about him as well, a sense of presence and power that clearly attracted all women.

She had seen the covert, wistful looks that Barbara cast at him, and the drawling flirtation that Kerry was beginning to aim in his direction. And when he had walked into the nightclub tonight, heads had turned at all the tables.

James, she was sure, was fully aware of these reactions, but he seemed to treat them lightly, as a predictable part of his everyday life. Just as he seemed to assume that any girl would welcome his embrace when he indulged a passing fancy to kiss her.

But none of that made her own reaction any easier to cope with. After all, her job brought her into contact with any number of bronzed and handsome suitors, yet none before had stirred the slightest interest in her. She was not in the market for any serious involvement—she knew only too well the heartache that that could bring—and she had never thought, until now, that mere physical attraction alone could so unsettle her.

But James did things to her pulses that had never happened to her before with such intensity. She no longer knew where she was with him, and she did not like it one bit.

The sound of slamming car doors interrupted her thoughts and made her heart sink. Any moment now the revellers would be bursting drunkenly in with demands for glasses and ice and more logs for the fire. She had hoped to be finished and in bed before they all got back.

But they dispersed surprisingly quickly and quietly. Maybe the first day on the slopes had shattered their stamina.

'Aha!'

'Oh, Ned,' she said wearily, trying to disengage the arm-lock that was suddenly flung about her waist. It was a grip like iron, and his breath on her cheek was wine-laden and made her want to retch. 'If you stay here you'll have to do something useful. Like dry all those plates.'

She screwed round in his arms and saw at once that rational conversation was beyond him. His eyes swam wetly, and his body slumped like a dead weight against her. If she did not get him to bed he was likely to pass out right here on the kitchen floor.

'Come on, Ned.'

'Where we going?'

'To your room.'

'Thought—never—ask,' he slurred.

She snorted. 'Come on, stand on your own feet.'

'Can't, Sarah, too tired.'

'Then bed's the best place.'

She put her arm round his waist and, closely entwined, they began a staggering progress towards the door. Although she was slight, she was both strong and determined, and after the first few stumbling feet Ned began to walk passably next to her.

They were making good progress across the main room to his bedroom door when the chink of glass made her start. In the shadows James stood at the corner bar, pouring himself a glass of mineral water.

'Ah, Brother James—thought we were alone——'

'So I see.' His eyes went straight past Ned to Sarah, taking in the way she held him close. 'This is a strange way to collect your thoughts.'

She returned his look silently.

Ned said, surprisingly lucidly, 'Well, can't stand here chatting. Got an appointment. With the pillows and sheets.'

'He's drunk.'

'Is he?' said James, holding her eyes with a look like cold steel. She felt it go through her, chilling every part of her. 'Well, I suppose that explains his behaviour. I wonder what explains yours.'

CHAPTER SIX

'LOOK, I know how it looked, but I did *not* sleep with Ned last night! I slept here, in my own bed! Alone!'

Sarah was not sure how it had happened, but somehow, within minutes of fumbling to switch off her shrilling alarm clock, she was engaged in a full-scale shouting match with James.

It was not yet seven o'clock, still dark outside, and she felt terrible. She was never at her best in the early mornings, and last night sleep had eluded her. She had tossed and turned, her body disturbed by James' touch and her mind restlessly reviewing the present and past.

Not for two years had thoughts of a man kept her awake, not since those terrible, dark three months when the man she'd thought she would marry had abruptly departed with a girl who had been until then one of her best friends, and night after night she had lain awake wondering how she was ever going to get through the rest of her life.

But then the job at NewSki had come along, and very quickly her life had become more full and interesting than she had ever imagined possible. It had been easy to ensure she was too busy to risk any involvement, and the possibility of being hurt that way again.

For that she had Gail and Brian to thank, and their seemingly limitless faith in her abilities, and that was something else she had reviewed in the dark hours of last night. Yet again she had renewed her vow to keep control of herself, and work even harder to keep their would-be buyer, and potential saviour, sweet.

But already she had broken that promise.

James had been coming out of his room, already shaved and dressed, as she blearily headed for the bathroom.

'Tired, Sarah?' There was a hard taunt in his voice that had stung her stretched nerves.

'I've been up half the night.'

'Oh?' A raised, mocking eyebrow had grated at her self-control.

'Clearing up and putting drunken guests to bed,' she snapped. She yanked the belt of her kimono tighter and saw his eyes flicker to the curves of her naked breasts under the thin cotton.

'And no doubt staying to hold their hands while they drifted off to sleep. Your devotion to my intemperate brother is quite touching—I can't help wondering just how far it goes——'

She ran a hand through her tousled hair and confronted him angrily. Her face was pale and her eyes hollow. She had not yet washed, had no make-up on and knew she must look a sight, yet her ragged morning temper made all that irrelevant.

Furiously she flared at him, throwing her arm out to indicate the rumpled single bed behind her from which she had just stepped.

'There, you see! The evidence. If you like you can go and examine it. You'll see there's only one dent on the pillow. Although why I should have to account to you for how I spend my nights is quite beyond me.'

His eyes followed hers to her room, going over

the scattered underwear she had tiredly shrugged off the night before flicking back to her.

This morning his glance was grey and palely chill, she saw, although his familiar profile was more disturbing than ever. 'I believe you. Apart from anything else, if Ned was as far gone as you claim. I can see he would be fit for nothing but twelve hours' heavy snoring.'

'Oh!'

She glared at him in disgust, but as she did so she saw that despite his freshly groomed appearance there were dark smudges under his eyes, too.

'You look as if you could do with a few more hours of that yourself,' she said bluntly. 'Were you up half the night as well—maybe checking for footsteps on the stairs?'

'I was, as it happens. Up half the night. Not checking footsteps, working. And now I'm in rather desperate need of some coffee before I tackle some important phone calls.'

'Well, you'll just have to wait. Breakfast will be at least half an hour——' She stopped abruptly, horrified at the snappish tone in her voice, and suddenly remembering the role she had been sent here to play. 'But if you can give me five minutes I'll bring you some down,' she finished lamely.

'Thank you, I would like that.' He responded with immediate civility to her change of tone, then his eyes sparked with open sexuality and he nodded at her robe. 'Especially if you serve it in that little Japanese geisha number. It's a very fetching sight first thing in the morning.'

But, when she knocked at his door soon after, he was so absorbed in scribbling notes he hardly seemed to notice her fresh outfit of lemon sweatshirt and black leggings, or the way she had brushed her hair up into a loose topknot and carefully applied her make-up.

'Here's your coffee. I've brought you a whole pot, and milk and sugar. I couldn't remember how you take it.'

'Thanks. Could you put it over there?'

She could have been any hotel waitress, she thought, for all the notice he took of her, and perversely she lingered at the door. She looked a hundred times better than she had done first thing and she wanted him to notice it.

After a moment he looked up, a dark, questioning glance.

'I was just thinking—it seems such a shame that you have to be stuck indoors all the time. Even if you didn't want to ski, you could take some of the lifts up to the mountain restaurants. The views are superb——' His eyes darkened with impatience and she swallowed nervously. 'It gets very hot in the sun. It's probably warm enough to sit and work, even on the higher terraces.'

He leant back and opened his fingers to let his pen drop with a small thud on his notepad. After a long silence he said, 'Tell me something. Are all the NewSki girls like you?'

She swallowed again, sure she had gone too far. 'What am I like?'

'Efficient. Bolshie. Interfering.'

'I didn't mean to interfere.'

He stood up and came towards her, talking over her words. 'Not to mention outrageously desirable,' his hand went up to her neck, her hair, but she saw cold anger in his eyes and reared away from the touch of his fingers, 'but with an ex-

cruciating taste in men——' he added insultingly
and dropped his hand and turned away.

'I don't know what you mean!'

'Ned is what I mean. It's quite beyond me what
someone like you, Sarah, sees in someone like
him!'

She opened her mouth to deny it absolutely, to
nail his misconceptions for once and all, but then
she remembered the dinner she had to cook tonight
and all the nights after that—inevitably he was
going to see the two of them together a great deal.

Her silence condemned her. Like a cornered
animal, she went instinctively on the attack.

'A lot of things seem to be beyond you! You
don't ski, and you don't consider this to be a
holiday! Why, millions of people would give their
right arms to spend two weeks here, in this chalet,
in this resort, at the height of the season, but you
seem to consider it purgatory! All you do is lock
yourself away and work. I doubt if you've even
looked out of the window for more than two
minutes. You might as well be in some city office
for all the pleasure the mountains give you!'

James' look was so grim, there was white about
his lips where he pressed them together. Then he
spoke lashingly. 'Don't you ever dare presume to
tell me what gives me pleasure and what doesn't!
And as for work, it's my work that allows everyone
else in this chalet to enjoy themselves, including
you, Miss Milner. I don't mind telling you that if
you're hoping for a job next season then you'd
better start watching your words. Not to mention
working on your tact and good manners, because
at the moment they fall very far short of the
standard that most employers would expect from

someone doing your job!'

She looked at him furiously, biting back the desire to tell him she would rather be out on the streets, penniless and hungry, than carry on being a general dogsbody for customers as rude and arrogant as himself.

A glacial 'I see,' was all she permitted herself, before turning at once to open the door.

Behind her she heard a sharp intake of breath, then James' voice, low and grim as she left the room. 'Oh, no, you don't,' he bit out. 'You don't see at all.' But she had no idea what he meant.

The next few days were among the longest of her life, but at last, at last it was Wednesday and a perfect sunny day for her day off.

She stood poised at the top of the mountain and looked down at the fresh white sweep of snow that curved away from her feet. The clear, sharp air filled her lungs, dispersing the cigar and alcohol fumes that seemed to fill the chalet, and all around her was absolute silence.

She felt her own self again, confident and independent, in control of her own life, and as she pushed off down the valley her blood pumped with exhilaration.

To hell with James and his brooding presence, she thought. To hell with twittering Barbara, and drawling Kerry and bothersome Ned! To hell with endlessly worrying about meals, and masking the real Sarah Milner behind a meek and blandly smiling domestic servant.

Not that it had been that bad, over the last few days, as the group had slowly shaken down into some sort of cohesion.

Barbara had gained confidence in her skiing, just

as Brad had predicted she would. Ned had been a brick as far as helping her out in the kitchen was concerned and had thankfully had his amorous attentions diverted by an increasing amount of time spent in Kerry's company. Tim continued as he had started, but she simply refused to take his drawling arrogance seriously.

As for James—the rhythm of her flawless skiing faltered—he had kept himself to himself and there had been virtually no contact between them, although she was acutely aware of his presence whenever they found themselves in the same room.

He spent a lot of time working, but once she had surprised him out on the balcony alone, his eyes lifted to the far peaks, with a strange, tense look of longing on his face.

At least, that was what it had seemed like in the brief glimpse she'd had of his expression before he masked it with his habitual cool stare. Only a dull flush of colour along his cheekbones had left her sure that, whatever it was she had seen, it had been private, and not something he chose to share with anyone.

But all that was far away, below her, in the valley. Up here she felt gloriously free of the hectic emotions that surged ceaselessly inside her. The sun shone, the snow sparkled, and she was alone on the mountain, a slight figure in a shocking pink ski-suit, a fur headband keeping her flying hair in place, her lips blotted with white zinc cream to keep away the rays which burned with ferocity up here in the thin, high air.

It was almost dark when she skidded to a halt at the bottom of the final run of the day. She felt exhausted but marvellous, fit and hungry, with her troubled mind at peace again. Up there in the mountains, she thought, she had managed to get in touch with herself again, and she felt newly healed and whole. And the best thing was that she still had hours of freedom.

She walked into town and pushed open the door of Jean's Bar, a popular tea-time rendezvous. Immediately arms waved, beckoning her over.

'Hi, boss!'

'Come and slum it with us!'

Other NewSki girls drew her into a big noisy circle of chalet girls and their clients, teasing her about her humble status. They knew nothing about her role, except that she had flown out to fill the sudden gap left by Annabel's illness, and she knew they admired her for rolling up her sleeves and plunging into what was a much tougher job than most outsiders appreciated.

'Had a good day, Sarah?'

'Fabulous, just fabulous!' She pulled off her headband and unzipped her jacket, flushed and sparkling. 'I went over to the other side of the valley. If you go to the top station and ski along to the left for a bit there's the most marvellous long run right down to the bottom village. It goes for miles and no one is ever on it——' For some moments she enthused radiantly about the glories of what she had for years considered to be her own private piece of the mountains.

'It's because it's too easy,' one of the other girls put in. 'There's that steep gully at the top which puts the beginners off, but after that it's tame. Most people who go up that high want to try their hands at the black runs.'

'Well, it suits me. It's where I always ski when

I'm here, and it's always empty. I love taking it slowly, looking at the scenery, thinking my own thoughts. To me that's what skiing is really all about. You can forget all that mogul bashing and hammering down ice fields. Just give me a nice gentle run, the breeze in my face, the smell of the pines——'

'Ah!' several of the girls said in chorus, and she laughed at their good-natured ribbing and reached for her mug of hot chocolate.

A young man sitting next to her bent towards her with an interested look she recognised all too well.

'You make it sound wonderful—I'd love to see it.'

She favoured him with a cheerful, impersonal smile. 'It is. But I'm afraid I'm not in the business of encouraging other people to go there. I like it to myself.'

The man sat back, deflated, and she felt guilty at the briskness of her put-down. After all, it wasn't his fault that his soft, blond features were not the dark good looks she craved to see.

For a moment she shut her eyes and let her thoughts linger on James, then she opened them, and there, as if her mind had conjured the man to reality, she suddenly saw him, sitting at the next table along.

At first he was just a blur, but she knew at once that it was him, could almost feel his vibrations in the air around her.

She turned a fraction more and saw that he was sitting alone, reading a financial newspaper, with a coffee and cognac in front of him. The other seats at his table were occupied, but she could see at once the group was nothing to do with him. There seemed to be a barrier around him that was far more solid than just the space between the chairs.

Exile, she thought again, and she surreptitiously pressed a hand to her side to calm the thumping of her surprised heart. I'm sure I'm right. He's in exile, cut off from everything around him, holding himself back, not allowing himself to come alive.

And as she looked at him, his isolation, she softened towards him so much that it was as if the heat of her gaze reached out to him, for he stirred in his seat, glanced towards her, then drank down his cognac and folded his paper.

She thought he was coming to talk to her, and she felt her heart leap up inside her ribs, but he only acknowledged her gaze with a curt nod.

'Sarah,' he said, in briefest greeting as he pushed his way past, yet something in his eyes told her that he had been watching her ever since she first made her way into the bar, exuding radiant health and happiness. And, although she could not have said why, she was sure it was because of her that he was now leaving.

Sitting so close, he had probably been able to hear every word of their conversation, and she sent up a private prayer of thanks that the talk had not strayed to her difficult chalet party.

'Hello, James,' she replied quietly, and she saw his glance sweep round the table before he pushed on towards the door, a dark figure and one of the very few not clad in skiing gear.

'Wow!' One of the girls whistled roundly. 'Who's that?'

'He looks familiar—he isn't in films or something, is he?' said someone else.

'That's James. James Holloway. He's in my

chalet.'

'I thought you said it was an awful group—he doesn't look a bit awful to me. Quite the opposite.'

'He might be good-looking, but that doesn't make him——' She stopped. She had been going to say he wasn't much fun, but suddenly she felt fiercely loyal towards him. And how could she be sure he was no fun, when she knew nothing about him at all?

'He's all right,' she said. 'It's the others who are so dreadful.' And for the next few minutes she entertained the company with wicked thumbnail sketches of their various foibles and follies.

It was dark before she left the bar and made her way through the frosty streets towards the main lift area from where the road went on up the hill to the chalet, and the ski slopes glimmered only faintly, silent and empty.

But something was happening that stopped her in her tracks.

She made her way forward. An ambulance was parked by the lift entrance, its light turning. A small knot of onlookers was standing nearby, while out of the darkness, with powerful electric torches lighting their path, came some figures skiing swiftly.

'What is it?' she asked someone.

'It's the blood wagon,' he said, using the grim slang term for the rescue stretcher used to bring injured skiers off the mountain. 'Some idiot was skiing off piste alone. It's taken them hours to get him down. Apparently it was a toss up whether to call the helicopter out to winch him off, or not.'

A horrible premonition flooded through her. Some idiot. She knew only too well who might be capable of that sort of thing.

As the stretcher was brought to a halt near the ambulance, she pushed her way on to the snow and crouched down to peer at the white face in its cocoon of blankets and foil sheeting.

Her fears were realised, as she had known they would be. Tim lay there, his eyes closed, his skin waxen.

'I know this man. He's in my chalet.' She spoke in rapid French to the rescuers. 'What has happened to him?'

The leader of the team spoke as he helped to lift the stretcher to the ambulance, telling her where he had been spotted, lying helpless in the snow. He had a broken leg, he said, and other injuries, but they did not know what. He'd lain for a long time before they'd got to him, and he was in poor shape.

'Sarah, what is it?'

She was somehow unsurprised to see James, but immensely relieved. She turned to him, her eyes anxious, her hands out. He took them unhesitatingly and his grip was firm and warm.

'It's Tim, he's had an accident. They'll have to take him down to the main hospital. They only do small things in the clinic here.'

'Is he badly hurt?'

She nodded. When one of the rescuers paused, she confirmed with him the hospital they were heading for.

'You are going with him?' the rescuer asked.

She turned to James. 'Someone should—maybe Kerry?'

'She'd be useless,' he said bluntly. 'And she hasn't got your French.'

She looked at him.

'Would you mind? I know it's your day off.'

'Mind? Of course not.'

She climbed into the ambulance and looked at Tim's unconscious figure. The sight frightened her. He looked as if he might easily die. James stood by the open doors and saw the look on her face.

'He looks terrible,' she said to him.

He hesitated for a moment, then he, too, stepped quickly up. 'I'll come as well,' he said decisively. 'We can ring the chalet from the hospital.'

Tim was whisked away from them the minute they finished the long and painfully slow journey down the mountain roads to the town. They waited in the casualty unit while the initial examination was made, then the nurse told Sarah he was going straight to the operating theatre.

'He's broken his pelvis, as well as his leg, and they've got to stop some internal bleeding,' she reported to James. 'They can't tell the full extent of the damage yet.'

'Come and have some coffee, you look terrible.' James steered her by the elbow to a chair in the waiting area. 'They'll come and find us when they've got anything to report.'

She sank down wearily, tugging at the buttons and zips of her skiing suit. The hospital was unbearably hot. It seemed a million years since she had been winging down the mountain in the frosty sunshine.

'I can't help feeling it's my fault,' she said miserably. 'I knew from the first day he was the kind of skier most likely to have an accident. I ought to have warned him, or fixed him up with a guide, or something.'

James took her hand, and again the feeling of his touch, so sure, was unbelievably comforting.

'He wouldn't have listened to you—don't forget, you're only the servant!' His mouth was crooked, trying to coax her out of her depression. He turned her hand in his, and abstractedly she looked down at his long, supple fingers, and then back at him, smiling wanly.

'Tim's always been too arrogant by half,' he said. 'It sounds cruel to say it, but he's had this coming for years. No one could have stopped it.'

'No, but maybe with a warning it needn't have been so bad.'

'Warnings mean nothing to people like him. He's always been reckless in everything he's done. Even in business. That's why he gave me a loan when no one else would.'

'You mean you were a lousy bet?'

'I was just starting out, I had no track record for people to go on.' He stood up. 'I ought to phone the chalet and tell them what's happened. Then I'll get you a coffee.'

'I'd rather have a drink of water. I'm boiling in this suit.'

'Take it off.'

'I can't. I've only got a T-shirt and tights underneath.'

'I'm sure that's perfectly decent.'

She shook her head.

'People would be shocked. It wouldn't seem proper. You don't know what these hospitals can be like.'

'I wouldn't be so sure of that,' he said enigmatically. 'Will you be all right for a few minutes?'

She nodded, and he went away, but without him she felt achingly alone and her fears for Tim crowded miserably in on her. To her relief he was soon striding back through the door.

'Any news?'

She shook her head. 'How did Kerry take it?'

His mouth twisted. 'I don't get the impression she cares a great deal for Tim, or indeed anyone except herself. She took the news with equanimity. Brad was more upset. If it's any comfort to you, he thinks it's his fault. Here——' He handed her a paper beaker of water and a bundle of white cloth.

'What's that?'

'A nurse's dress. I managed to borrow it for you. To save you sweltering away in all that thermal insulation. The cloakroom's down the corridor.'

She took it, moved by his thoughtfulness, and put it on. It was miles too big, and the front gaped open while the sleeves hung down over her wrists. She arranged it as best she could, borrowing the belt from her skiing suit, but it still swamped her slight frame and made her look like an orphaned refugee. She returned to her seat feeling foolish. James' scrutiny was close, increasing her embarrassment, but when he spoke his voice was warm.

'Mmm. Uniforms are supposed to be sexy—but in this case——' Yet in spite of his words there was a something in his eyes she had not seen there before, an unmasked look of wanting, almost shy, that made a hot warmth unfurl beneath her ribs.

'It feels much better,' she said, determinedly practical. The warmth slowly subsided as she stared at her feet. The moment passed. She wriggled her toes, glad to be free of her woollen tights and heavy ski boots, and felt cool air on her legs. 'It was thoughtful of you. Thank you very much.'

He was looking at her legs. 'Brown face, pale legs,' he said lightly. 'A skier's tan. And speaking of which——' he leant forward and with his handkerchief gently wiped her lips '—that white sun block looks very odd under these neon lights. Ghostly——'

She licked her lips, and he watched the pink tip of her tongue outlining the shape of her mouth as if he could not take his eyes from her face.

Then the door swung open as two nurses walked through the room, and she frowned at her ankles, worrying again about Tim.

Determinedly he began to distract her. 'Where did you learn your excellent French? You speak it like a native.'

'At university. I took a degree in modern languages.'

'And then?'

'Then I did a year's course in business studies in London. I had a notion I might work in Europe for a time, for the European Community or the Council of Europe.'

'And did you?'

She shook her head. 'Things got in the way.'

'Let me guess—a boyfriend?'

She grinned a little, embarrassed. 'Is it such a predictable story? I suppose it is. He took a job in the north of England, and he didn't want me taking off across the Channel without him. Like a fool, I agreed.' Her voice twisted.

'What happened?' His voice was very low and easy. 'If you want to talk about it, of course——'

They were sitting side by side, so close she could feel the warmth of his body, and she suddenly found words spilling out with surprising ease.

'We were both doing the same diploma course, although he was older than me. He'd already had five years out in the world. He seemed very mature and certain of what he wanted, at least compared to all the people I'd known at university.

'We were together the whole year. In the end I moved in with him. We didn't actually get engaged, but we both assumed we would stay together and get married at some point. We talked about buying a house, even having a family at some time in the future . . .'

She stared unseeingly across the room, remembering how safe and certain life had seemed then.

'We knew each other's families, took holidays together. Why, we even went skiing together, in Austria. We were as married as it's possible to be without actually having rings on our fingers.'

Again there was the bitter edge of betrayal in her voice.

James prompted her. 'But——'

'It all started to go wrong in the summer, when we were both looking for work. He came home one day and announced out of the blue that he'd taken a job in Manchester. I remember feeling very hurt that he hadn't told me about the interview or consulted me about his decision.' She turned to James', her eyes angry with the memory. 'That was our first major row. After that I decided I would go off to Europe, as I'd originally intended to do, and get a year or so's experience working in another language, but he wouldn't hear of it. He

said we'd never manage to keep the relationship
going, that we would just drift apart.'

'So you went off to Manchester.'

'I started to look for jobs there. He moved
north, and I stayed in London to wind up our flat
and pack our things. The day before I planned to
join him he telephoned me to say not to come. He
said there was someone else.' To her horror, there
was a break in her voice as the awfulness of that
night returned to her. James touched her hand and
the words came out in a rush. 'But it wasn't just
someone, it was a friend of ours—of mine—from
the course. One of my closest friends. That was the
worst thing of all,' she went on flatly, 'that
everyone had let me down. I found out later that
they'd been having an affair all summer, lots of
people knew about it, and she'd actually followed
him up to Manchester to be with him.'

James said nothing, although his lips were
pressed together as if he felt her old pain, and she
was glad of his silence. After a time she turned to
him, willing him to understand.

'It wasn't the break-up of the affair that was so
bad. When I finally got used to the idea, I even
realised it was for the best. The warning signals for
the relationship were already there. It was the
underhandedness of it all, the deception of my
girlfriend, and the way they had both let me
abandon my own plans, even though they must
have known by then it was for nothing. After that I
decided I would make all my own decisions in
future, and let no one get in the way of them ever
again.'

'And let no one get close to you ever again,'
James echoed quietly, as his eyes read the hurt on

her face.

She held his eyes but a flush tinged her cheeks.
'It wasn't deliberate. I'm not quite as tough as
that. It just seemed easier to throw myself into my
job. And, anyway, if you happen to work for a ski
company you soon get to feel pretty cynical about
the average relationship. You wouldn't believe the
amount of bed-hopping that goes on in most
chalets! And it's often the couples who seemed
most happy and settled together who are the worst.
On bad nights it can be like living in a French
farce.'

She wriggled her toes together, staring at her feet
and remembering her early innocence when she had
been both shocked and disbelieving at some of the
things she had seen on her flying visits to resorts.

'You don't approve of all that?' He was smiling
at her, coaxing her back from her black memories
with gentle mockery. She didn't care. It felt so
comfortable sitting here, next to him, talking to
make the time pass.

She shrugged. 'I'm no prude. But it doesn't seem
to make people very happy, and it's not for me.'

She thought about James and his girlfriend, the
one Ned had replaced at the last minute on this
skiing trip, and wondered how much bed-hopping
he liked to indulge in. But the thought of him in
bed made a hungry hollow open up inside her chest
until she had to swallow and get up to pace the
room, hugging the white uniform around her. And
even then she could feel his eyes upon her, as if he
knew full well the feelings that had driven her from
her seat, and her restlessness did not go away.

How could she have thought him comfortable?

Sexual tension surged up like a tide between them at every opportunity.

Then a nurse came hurrying in, looking for them. Sarah went to her and they spoke at length.

James came forward. 'I got the rough gist of that,' he said, as the nurse went away, 'but you'd better fill me in on the details.'

'They've done what they can at this stage. He's in intensive care, but they think he'll be OK. She said he's stable and unless something entirely unexpected happens, he'll pull through all right. The bleeding wasn't as bad as they feared, although his pelvis is broken in two places. She said he'll need an air ambulance to get home—but that shouldn't be a problem if his insurance is in order. I'll ring London about it tomorrow.'

She thought she was speaking matter-of-factly, completely in control, but suddenly, as she spoke, her knees began to shake and tremble. To her dismay, she felt her throat tighten and tears well into her eyes.

As the news that Tim wasn't going to die sank home, all her bottled-up anxiety surged forward. She had needed to stay cool and calm, but now she could not retain control any longer. Her voice faltered and caught, and then sobs were racking her, her hands hanging helplessly at her sides.

'Oh, Sarah! Sarah,' James said, his voice ragged, and he stepped forward and wrapped his arms tight about her, holding her close while the crying storm raged, his cheek moving like a caress against her hair. 'It's all right,' he said, again and again. 'It's all right, it's all right.'

But her sobs went on and on, and after a time it seemed as if she were crying for everything, not just Tim, but for all the hurt and rejection she had carried inside her for so long. Leaning against James' shoulder, she wept it all away against his strength.

As the shaking gradually eased he moved one hand to stroke the back of her head and down to the hollow of her slender neck, over and over rhythmically soothing her, while she felt his solidity and warmth reviving her shaken spirit.

She didn't fight his embrace. The comfort of it was more than she could have dreamt of. She closed her eyes and leaned her forehead against his chest and breathed in the warm male closeness of him like life-giving oxygen. Gradually her shoulders stopped trembling, and he tipped her chin gently up and looked down at her, his eyes dark and certain.

'I thought he was going to die.' Somehow she managed to find a small, apologetic smile. Her cheeks were wet and her eyes felt swollen, but she knew he would not judge her for that.

'You don't have to apologise. Or explain.'

He did not let her go, but as they stood holding each other, looking long into each other's eyes, the nature of their embrace changed. A charge seemed to run between them, stirring his desire against her, and setting her own body beating in response.

He shifted his weight imperceptibly to hold himself a little back from her, but his arms still steadied her. One hand moved to ease back her tousled hair from her cheek. Her eyes were bright, her lashes clumped with tears. For a moment he did not speak, then he said hoarsely, 'I think I'll take back what I said about that uniform. It's very, very disturbing.'

She met his eyes and then had to look quickly away from what she saw there.

'I'll go and change,' she began, but his arm tightened as she tried to move away and he bent to kiss her with such a force of passion that she turned instantly back to him, moving instinctively within his arms to answer his lips.

How long they stood like that she neither knew nor cared. Their last kiss, out in the dark night, had been a fruitless fight to get close. Now they were close, but they strove to get closer.

His lips opened hers, seeking and finding, and his hands came up impatiently to part the gaping neck of her ill-fitting uniform and find the soft, swelling skin beneath.

'Oh!' She gasped at what he made her feel. She forgot it was a hospital, a public place, and moved beneath his hands, searching to pull him against her.

But, abruptly as he had kissed her, so he pulled away, leaving her body beating and her head spinning. She opened her eyes in shock. His eyes were bright, his hair tousled and he breathed fast and hard.

For a moment he still held her, then his hands dropped. He ran a hand through his hair, and turned away, recovering. And when he spoke he said simply, 'I'll get a taxi to take us back. Meet me by the front door.'

Going back, on the long tortuous journey up the winding mountain road as the meter clicked up a small fortune in fares, they sat apart, absorbed in their own thoughts.

It was as if they had collided by accident, she thought. As if they had cannoned together with such unexpected and unwelcome force that the shockwaves of it had thrust them immediately apart again.

She glanced covertly at James, but he had the black collar of his coat turned up against the cold, and his eyes, flicking over the passing snowy darkness, gave no clue to his thoughts.

She sighed silently and turned back to her own side of the car. She hadn't wanted this to happen, and from the look on his face she guessed he felt much the same. But it had happened. There was no denying it. There had been more savage wanting in their kiss than she had ever known before, and, despite her scathing words about the bed-hopping of chalet guests, she knew that if James chose to pursue what was happening between them she would have no will to resist him.

And if he chose not to—she sighed again—if that happened, she wasn't sure she could bear it.

The taxi stopped and James paid with a folded bundle of notes. They crunched across the snow to the chalet in silence. The place was dark.

'No one's even bothered to wait up,' she said.

James, shutting the door behind them, did not reply. There was an awkward pause, during which she felt his gaze, unfathomable on her back.

'You haven't eaten,' she said, remembering her duties. 'Would you like me to make you an omelette or something?'

'I'm not hungry.'

'Then perhaps I'd better get some sleep—it is the middle of the night, after all.' She took a step towards her room, aching for him to prevent her going. There seemed to be vast oceans of unspoken words between them, setting the air humming with tension.

'I need a brandy.' He was shrugging off his coat, but his eyes were on her, and she could sense in his look a silent inner struggle with himself. 'Why don't you join me?'

She scrutinised his eyes. 'You don't really want me to,' she said. 'You're just being polite.'

'Let me be the judge of what I want to do, or not do. If I hadn't wanted to, I wouldn't have asked you.' His voice was harsh, echoing the struggle in his look.

'Thank you, then. I'll just get out of these ski things.'

She changed quickly into her habitual leggings and sweatshirt, resisting a powerful impulse to wear anything more seductive. Despite his curt words, or maybe because of them, she was more certain than ever that he was attracted to her despite himself, and had no real appetite for a holiday entanglement.

He stoked the dying embers of the fire and poured drinks. It was very cosy in the warm room, comfortably cluttered with books and magazines, but quiet except for the occasional splutters from the fire. James took a seat by the fire. She sat cautiously on the other side of the fire, on the floor, back against a chair and her knees drawn up to her chin.

'Tell me when you started skiing,' he said, after a time.

'When I was just ten. My grandmother started me off, would you believe? She was a marvellous old lady, one of those old-time Alpine skiers with knickerbockers and lace-up boots. She used to come down the mountains very slowly, but very surely, with a wonderful smile on her face. My parents never took to it, but I went off with her every winter, and she made sure I went into ski school each year and learned the basics thoroughly. Then she'd take me off skiing with her and we'd go for miles.

'It was wonderful, but all very sedate. There was always time to think about your skiing, and to look at the view. Later, when I started going with friends, I fell into the trap of trying to outdo them all by being the fastest and the most reckless.' She smiled at him. 'Then I ruined one holiday by pulling my knee on the first day and I had a lot of time on my hands to think about my foolishness!'

'But it didn't put you off skiing?'

'No, it wasn't very serious, I went back the next year and had no problems. When I joined NewSki I couldn't believe my luck—being paid to pursue my greatest passion.'

He turned his mouth down wryly. 'I'm not sure spending all night in a hospital casualty department can be classed as luck. Nor having to look after a chalet party like this one.'

'I don't often spend nights at the hospital, and in a week or so you'll all be gone. It's a small price to pay.'

She spoke crisply because his eyes on her were starting the hollow feeling inside her chest again, and she did not want to feel that way for him, any more than she suspected he wanted to feel the same attraction for her.

He wasn't her kind. She had to remember that. They had nothing in common, except the sexual tension that had grown out of nowhere to drag them relentlessly towards each other. And surely they were both mature enough to manage to resist it? Surely?

He lifted an eyebrow and swallowed his brandy. 'That's true. And then what? After us?'

She shrugged, instantly guarded. 'I don't know, probably back to London.'

'They called you "boss", the girls in the bar.' His voice was a challenge.

'It was a joke. I've just got more experience than them.' She spoke too quickly, and he knew it.

'Sarah——'

She looked at his long frame, legs extended from the chair, and spoke impulsively, blocking the probing question she was sure was coming. 'You know, I can really hardly believe you don't ski. I'm sure you'd be a natural. You seem to be fit——'

Now it was his turn to speak rapidly, angrily. 'I'm perfectly fit. I swim almost daily, I play squash and tennis, I just don't ski. Leave it. Sarah. I've told you before. You're not going to convert me, so don't waste your energies trying!'

She looked as him, wide-eyed. 'I'm sorry.' His eyes had grown dark, now they stayed dark, the grey of fury slowly turning a warmer blue, his look meeting hers until she felt her mouth grow dry. She swallowed the last of her drink and got up quickly, reeling a little with tiredness. 'I think I'd better go to bed, if you'll excuse me——'

He got up easily and lithely from the chair, so that he was standing close to her. She felt his closeness, like warmth against her skin, even though they were not touching. But then they were, because he had reached for her hands and turned them to him.

'No,' he said quietly. 'I'm the one who should

say sorry. There was no reason to get angry like that. Especially when you've done so much today, and you're so tired.'

She looked up at him, sure he would feel how she was shaking at his touch. His hands were strong and firm, holding her confidently.

'I——' she began uncertainly, but she stopped. Her heart was thudding a drumbeat of desire, her lips were parted and her eyes were wide, showing clear and white against dark lashes.

James shook his head slightly, as if in disbelief at the way she looked, and his own weakness in needing her. Then his head bent and his lips found hers slowly, in a gentle, exploratory kiss that quickly deepened as he drew her close to him, his arms going round her to pull her closer still.

'Oh!' She gasped at the feeling of his lips on hers, the way they held all the complexity and held-in desire that she had sensed in him, and her mouth parted readily to his as they moved together, her hands holding the width of his shoulders and her head tilted up to receive him more fully.

It was more than she could have imagined, a million times more. It was wonderful, and it was devastating, and she wanted it never to end, but suddenly it did because a door abruptly opened, and there was Ned, blinking and smiling and saying nastily, 'Well, well, well! So you've decided to bestow your favours on Big Brother as well, have you, Sarah? A real family affair!'

CHAPTER SEVEN

IT WAS two days later and Sarah was riding the main lift to the top of the mountain, feeling the fragile cabin swing and tremble as it rose silently over the precipices and sparkling slopes below.

She held her skis between her knees and rested her forehead against them as she watched the scenery appear and disappear below her. Her cheeks were flushed, her eyes bright and her feelings swung as unsteadily as the car that ferried her aloft.

It was exactly like having a fever, she reflected. One minute she felt hot and excited, the next frozen and frightened, and her mood swooped and dipped without rhyme or reason.

She had not slept well since the night Ned had walked in on their embrace and James had walked instantly out, and the lack of rest was showing. This morning, noting her pale face and dark-rimmed eyes and the number of times she fumbled and dropped cutlery or plates as she served breakfast, James had said curtly, 'Sarah, for goodness' sake take a day off. And that's an order. You look as if you need it.'

'But——'

'But nothing. We can manage.'

'Oh, but James, we'll need tea when we come in this afternoon.' Kerry turned brown doe eyes on him. 'And what about dinner tonight—or rather supper, I believe the correct term would be for the kind of food we get served here.'

Ned looked outraged to have his cooking so demeaned, but Sarah had barely bothered to note his expression. Her eyes had been on James, whose own look as he had spoken to her had been devoid of any emotion.

'We'll go out. I'm sure Sarah will be glad of a break.'

There had been no point protesting. She knew that what he had really meant was that he would be glad of a break from the stifling atmosphere of the chalet, where it was impossible for the two of them not to trip over each other at every turn.

Although, since that night, they had both tried hard enough. One glance at him the next morning, his masked and shuttered expression, had told her all she needed to know.

What had happened the day before at the hospital, and then later, had been, for him, a mistake, a momentary aberration brought on by the strange circumstances, and the illusion of closeness that had grown between them as they waited tensely for news of Tim.

And she was relieved, she told herself firmly, because she did not want an involvement with one of her clients, not even someone as handsome and charismatic as James, any more than he wanted one with her. In fact, especially not someone like James, whose life touched hers at no recognisable point, and whose only response to the glorious Alpine scenery that she was now looking down on was to snap open his briefcase and bury his head in paperwork.

Except that the mountains seemed finally to be exerting their pull on him, for later that same morning, as she had headed from the kitchen to begin making beds in the upstairs rooms, she had again caught a glimpse of him on the balcony.

The sight made her step falter. He was a dark figure, alone, his face lifted to the sun which was climbing steadily in a crisp blue sky, his eyes on the fabulous panorama of peaks which rose far above the resort. The snow was dazzling and his eyes were creased against its glare, but the rest of his face might have been carved in stone for all the expression on it. His hands were pushed down into his pockets and he stood unmoving.

And yet—she stood staring—despite his stillness she sensed a yearning in him, a tension like a dog straining hard against a leash, quivering with held-in passion, and she longed to go to him and put her arms around him and urge him to loosen whatever bonds were holding him so fast.

But she forced herself to go on. After all, it was none of her business, none whatsoever. And, by the time she had finished her chores, James had left the chalet.

Not that that had meant her problems for the day were over, for in the hallway, tightening his ski boots, she bumped into Ned.

'It *boeuf en daube* tonight,' he told her. 'With smoked trout pâté to start and a *bavaroise* to follow.'

'Oh. That sounds complicated.'

He grinned lasciviously up at her. 'Just follow my instructions, slave, and you won't go wrong.'

'I'm not your slave,' she said indignantly.

'Maybe not. But I certainly expect as much— shall we say, submission?—as I noticed you giving Brother James last night.'

'That's none of your business!'

'No. I'm sure it was just a momentary madness,' he continued nonchalantly. 'After all, Brother James' eyes are turning in a different direction this morning.'

He glanced slyly up at her, but she steeled herself to say nothing.

'I mean, he didn't *have* to go to hospital with Kerry to visit Tim. You'd think he'd seen enough of that place last night to last a lifetime. But no. One pleading request from those pouting lips, one tremulous hand on his arm, one look from those spaniel eyes and he's fetching his coat and calling a taxi as meekly as anything.'

'That wouldn't be sour grapes talking, by any chance?' she said tightly.

'Sour grapes?'

'I seem to remember someone else responding with alacrity to those spaniel eyes. Now I suppose she's turned you down——'

'Turned me down?' Ned looked up and his eyes were full of mocking wickedness. 'Who said she turned me down? Quite the opposite, in fact. Kerry doesn't waste time—and she felt quite lonely last night.'

'Oh!' She guessed he spoke the truth and she turned away, sickened by this latest turn of the sexual merry-go-round she had witnessed in action all too often.

'Shocked, Sarah? Surely not. Chalet girls have seen it all before.'

'That doesn't mean we have to like it.' Her voice was curt.

'Kerry was very upset about Tim's accident. She needed a shoulder to cry on.' His eyes were callous, laughing. She could see he loved to play games and did not care who got hurt, or why.

'I can't waste time talking. I've got a million things to do.'

'Well, I hope you're not pining for James. He specifically said they wouldn't be back till late. I expect he and Kerry will need time to relax together after a hard day's hospital visiting——'

'Oh, stop it!'

'Sorry. Have I upset you? I'll tell you what. I'm meeting Brad and Barbara at the Alpine Bar for lunch. Why don't you play hookey for a couple of hours and join us? A few drinks, a gentle ski back down to the village—it'll set you up for the rest of the day.'

'Thanks, but no, thanks. I think I'll be tied up all day—making trout pâté.' Her voice twisted. She was only making all this culinary effort to impress James, yet he would be out wining and dining with Kerry. And she had already seen quite enough of how that particular lady operated to know that it would be a very predatory meal indeed. Inside her, her heart had lurched painfully at the thought, although she had managed to retain an illusion of outer calm . . .

The lift clanged into its final station at the top of the mountain. She got out and carried her skis off, lowering each one with a satisfying thump on to the snow. She stepped into first one, then the other, feeling the bindings snap into place, adjusted her gloves and ski poles, and began to ski gently along the narrrow track that led to her secluded favourite run.

James and Kerry had stayed out all day, and all evening too. She had been in bed by the time they'd returned, well past midnight, with Kerry's throaty laugh counterpointing the sound of slamming taxi doors.

She had lain alert, trying to guess from the footsteps and closing doors what was going on, but Brad and Barbara had still been up and the voices and noises mingled into a tangled muddle.

Later she'd definitely heard James' door open and close, but whether he had been alone or not, she hadn't been able to tell.

In the morning there had been no sign of Kerry when everyone else assembled for breakfast, James reported that Tim was in a much better state, although still in much pain, and followed her into the kitchen to confer on arrangements for the air ambulance.

Her bad temper, coupled with his unsettling closeness, had made her drop knives and bang plates, and it was then that he had scrutinised her pale face and ordered her to take time off.

And he had been right, she thought, as she skilfully negotiated the steep gully that led on to the run. It was icy this morning, and she had to concentrate hard to find the right moment to turn and the best places to find a grip. All her thoughts focused on the feeling of the mountain beneath her skis, the flexible bending and balancing of her slim body and the pure cold air that cleared her head and put pointless worries behind her.

As she came out of the gully she slowed and stopped, leaning on her poles to survey the scene which opened out ahead. This was the moment she loved the best, the pause and the anticipation before she pushed herself off and began the long swinging journey to the bottom.

It was almost midday. The sun was high. She narrowed her eyes behind her dark glasses and felt a welcome small breeze stir her hair. It carried with it the smell of the pines, from much further down the slope and she looked forward with pleasure to the narrow track which would lead her, fast, through their scented shade.

She took a deep breath. This was better. Out here, high on the slopes, a slight figure in her pink suit and fur headband, confident and sure, she was her own person again. James Holloway was nothing to her.

So what if his eyes made her heart beat unsteadily and his look made her mouth go dry? It was a passing fancy, nothing more. Next week he would be gone, but the mountain would still be here, and she would be free to ski, free to carry on enjoying her life, in her own way, without the unwanted hindrance of any ill-fated yearnings towards a man whose whole life seemed to be a negation of everything she held dear.

With the back of her gloved hand she pushed her glasses more firmly on to her nose and looked down the run ahead. To her intense annoyance she saw another skier ahead of her.

Occasionally this happened, but not very often, and she had grown used to expecting blessed solitude on what she saw as her own private ski run.

She swore mildly under her breath and lifted her poles from the snow, waiting for the skier ahead to put a reasonable distance between the two of them.

At last the black-clad figure disappeared over the first shoulder of the run. Only when that happened, and the scene was empty again, did she launch herself forward.

There must have been a light snowfall in the night, she realised, because, although parts of the run were mushy where the sun had begun to melt the surface, most of it was crisp and fresh beneath her skis.

She read the snow ahead of her as a sailor would read the sea, looking instinctively for turning points and hearing the new snow squeak and creak beneath her flashing skis. As she sped along her tensions evaporated, grey rags of bad temper torn away, and she felt power and sureness in everything she did.

Some days were just like this. No matter what you did, you could not put a ski wrong. But today was an extra bonus. She had not expected to be skiing, and she certainly had not expected to find herself able to rise above her worries so that she glided over the slopes like a magical winged creature.

At the first ridge she paused and the magic paled. The other skier was still there, only a short way ahead. Whoever it was must be a stumbling beginner, she realised, making only slow and painful progress—although if that was the case they must have had the greatest difficulty negotiating the ice gully at the top of the run.

She watched critically, but the figure was no beginner. He—now she was closer, she could see it was a man—was an expert, carving a sure and certain path.

Then, as she watched, he reached a bend in the run and stopped, skidding round so that he faced back up the slope towards her. From where he stood she would appear as a black silhouette against the sun, and she grinned a little grimly to herself as she imagined how his irritation would match her own when he realised he was not alone.

She waited, but he showed no signs of moving, so eventually she launched herself once again, knees bending gracefully as she swooped from one side of the run to the other.

The man made no move, but watched as she skied closer. She could see he was dressed in black and sat easily on his skis, like a professional.

Well, if he wouldn't get out of her way, she would get out of his, she thought, and took a steeper route down the slope, flashing past him on the far side of the slope. That was better. Ahead was the peaceful emptiness she had come to expect here, and she skied stylishly and well, trying to think of nothing but the moment.

But there was that man again, skiing past her and on down the mountain, disrupting any sense of harmony. She watched as he moved ahead. Although he was not skiing fast, she could see he was a tall figure, whose greater weight pushed his skis faster than hers.

She stopped and watched him. He was well worth watching. His skiing was superb, every moment in balance, and a spare economy of style that was beautiful to observe. His skis were the long, slender ones of the expert, but they were as close together as if stuck by glue, and his body bent and swayed to the mountain as if he had lived on it all his life.

She sighed. After years of watching skiers of all ages and abilities, there were very few who made her feel like this, as if she had barely learnt the rudiments of the art. But when she saw such perfection, it toughened her resolve to try harder, and harder still, to get better at the sport she loved.

The man had paused again, and again he was looking back up the slope. It was almost as if he were waiting for someone. She looked round. Maybe the rest of his group were about to come swarming over the hill. Maybe he was a local guide, or an instructor leading a party on the less-used parts of the mountain, and that was why he was here, on her own private slope, because the gentle run was certainly not very taxing to his obvious abilities.

She looked round, but there was no sound of anyone else coming down. She looked back to the man, and suddenly had the strange but certain feeling that it was her, and her alone, he was awaiting.

Underneath her warm clothing, her skin prickled. She had felt like this before in recent days. James made her feel that way, when she looked as him and had felt sure she sensed his hidden tensions, his sense of exile.

James.

She looked again at the figure ahead. A tall, dark man, with thick dark hair. A stance that was somehow familiar.

James! It couldn't be. She leant forward, as if an inch or two of difference would help her see his face.

There was no way—— James didn't ski—— The man could be anybody—— Why, sometimes it was hard enough to recognise your closest friends under their ski-suits and hats and goggles.

Not that this man wore a hat or goggles—just sunglasses, like her, to protect his eyes.

James. She shook her head angrily. Surely she was going crazy? She had James on her mind like water on the brain. Just because the man was tall, and had black, straight hair.

But it was nothing to do with his height or his hair, but the feeling she had when she looked at him, as if their two figures, so far apart on the slope, were linked. As if she could feel what he was feeling, and sense what he was sensing, and be drawn to him as certainly as she was now pushing herself forward, her skis gliding down the slope, bringing her inexorably closer to him.

Yet when she got nearer, he turned and skied on, slightly ahead, skiing slowly and levelly, so she could easily keep pace with him, although his face remained hidden from her.

And then somehow, without words, they were skiing together, bodies dipping and turning in unison, their skis whipping up sprays of powder as they skidded round, and the run no longer spoilt for her by this mysterious man's presence, but enchanced by his glorious skiing.

She held her thoughts suspended, lost in the joy of the perfect harmony of the two of them. Whoever the man was, it did not matter. All that mattered was the sheer joy of this strange duet, out here in the glittering white silence of the mountains.

Where the run dipped into a band of pine trees, the track became narrow and icy and they sped in single file through the silent, scented forest, the only sound the hiss of their skis on the ice until, eventually, they emerged into a wide bowl of un-trammelled snow, a beautiful valley that wound round and down the mountainside.

Without pause the mysterious skier went on, skiing high to the side of the valley before flicking his skis around to travel back to the far side. She followed him unhesitatingly. It was how she liked to ski this valley, like being on a glorious big dipper, up and down, feeling all the joy of rhythm and effortless motion. Now she hardly saw him, except as a black stroke of movement against the dazzle of the snow, but she knew he was there, knew they moved together, feeling the same springing joy at the snow, the sun, the scene, and their own place in it.

At last they reached the end of the valley. From here, she knew, there was a short, steep descent to where a small bar and restaurant marked the bottom of the run. She thought he might pause before this last stretch, or might even disappear away to the left, where a small trail led back down to the main valley and its huge network of runs. But he did neither. As she swung out of the valley she saw him speed away, cutting a much faster path down the slopes than before. She stopped to watch, knowing she could no longer keep pace with the speeding figure whose skis were now hammering over the snow, jumping bumps and skidding into expert turns.

When he reached the bottom she skied more sedately down the slope, and her heart began to knock with apprehension. Back up there, up on the mountain, among the snowfields, it had all been a dream, a weaving of bodies and minds that needed no words. But now . . .

The man had turned to face her, and again there was the prickle of foreknowledge on her skin. She knew who he was, and yet she didn't know because it simply couldn't be true and she was sure her mind must be playing tricks on her.

To stave off the moment of truth, she watched her skis, bringing herself easily to a stop near the dark figure that she only allowed herself to see from the corner of her eye.

Then she took a deep breath, tossed her hair back and looked up.

'You!'

James smiled at her, but it wasn't the James she knew, not the tense, moody man with the forbidding manner and his head permanently buried in a sheaf of papers.

This was another man, hair tousled, breath coming hard, face whipped by the wind.

Her thoughts tumbled in confusion. He looks ten years younger, she thought. Then, I hadn't known slate-blue eyes could be so warm. Then, urgently, how I want him!

'You can't ski!' she said accusingly.

He shook his head and grinned. His teeth against his tan were as white as the snow all around.

'That's not what I said. I said I *don't* ski. There's a difference.' His breath was ragged. He shook his head and mopped his forehead with the back of one hand. 'Phew. I'm really out of condition.'

It was her turn to shake her head. 'I don't understand. I mean . . .' She gestured at him. 'You didn't have any gear or anything.'

He held his hands wide, looking at his black racing gear, boots and skis.

'There's no mystery about that. I hired it all this morning. A sudden impulse.'

'I still don't understand. I can't get used to the

idea . . .' Her voice tailed away.

James laughed at her confusion, a full, carefree laugh that lit his face and melted something deep within her. I don't understand and I don't care, she thought. I just want him to kiss me!

But the impulse was obviously not shared. James gestured at the bar.

'Is that tumbledown heap of planks what I think it is? Can we get a drink there?'

'Yes. And lunch, if you're hungry.'

'Ravenous. I'd forgotten what mountain air does to the appetite.'

They skied to the door and took off their skis and loosened their boots. All his gestures were easy, almost habitual, she noticed. He was not just a good skier, he was someone who had lived on skis, found them as natural and normal as ordinary footwear.

He hustled her in, a hand on her arm, and ordered hot, spiced wine. They were the only people in the steamy room, and the proprietor eyed them hopefully.

'Will you have lunch?' he asked Sarah, whom he recognised.

'Yes, please.' She turned to James. 'The steak is excellent.'

'Steak, then. With mountains of chips! But only a few of these.' He lifted his glass at her with a cheerful wink.

'You're like a different person,' she told him, as they unzipped their jackets and settled into a corner alcove. 'I can't get used to it. I'm sorry if I keep staring at you.' You're also impossibly handsome, she thought, and I'm finally beginning to understand that what has been going on between us from the first is not quite as crazy as I thought it was.

'Not a different person,' he said. 'Myself. I can't tell you how much I've loathed sitting in that chalet for the past week.'

'Why on earth did you do it?'

He lifted his glass and drained it at one go, eyes on hers.

'You look beautiful sitting there—windswept and sparkling. And have I told you what a very good skier you are?'

She flushed with pleasure, but refused to be deflected. 'Not one twentieth as good as you— what's the story?'

He shrugged. 'I used to ski a lot.' He paused. 'All the time, really. Then I had an accident, a bad one. My left leg is entirely held together with nuts and bolts and any other pieces of old metal that the surgeons could lay their hands on. After a year of operations, and then more operations to undo the mistakes of the previous operations, and therapy of every kind they could think of, they pronounced that I could get back on skis again—provided I didn't do anything foolish like go fast and hard down a mountain.'

He eyed her. 'I was younger than I am now, foolish and pig-headed. To me skiing was all about going to the limit, beating everyone—including myself. I decided that if I couldn't ski the way I wanted to, I certainly wasn't going to go up and down the easy run like some doddering grandad. So I sold all my gear, declared myself an official non-skier and turned all my energies elsewhere. It worked—provided I kept away from the slopes——'

'And then you came on a skiing holiday.'

'Not a holiday, I told you. A business trip. I thought I could handle it. After all, my work had taken me in and out of resorts in America, and I hadn't felt too bad about not skiing. I didn't know this resort, so it held no memories for me, and I knew the company wasn't going to be congenial enough to make me feel I was missing out on the general sport. But it all proved harder than I expected.'

Sizzling steaks were brought to their table on wooden platters, accompanied by huge dishes of fresh chips. They both ate hungrily.

'Why?' she asked him. 'Why was it harder?'

He gestured at the mountains outside the window. 'This mainly. The magic of the Alps. And you.'

'Me?' Her eyes went to his, wide open in surprise.

'Do you remember the other afternoon, in Jean's Bar? When you were extolling the delights of this run to the assembled company? And giving them the benefit of your philosophy of skiing, just for good measure?'

She nodded, embarrassed. 'I don't often go on like that.'

'I couldn't help but eavesdrop, and everything you said seemed to get right under my skin. You could have been talking directly to me. I began to realise how stupid I was being, cutting myself off from all that just because I couldn't carry on exactly as before. Your view of it all seemed so much more mature than my adolescent pique.'

She flushed deeper, then flashed a shy look up. 'I'm glad to have been of service!'

'There was something else as well.' His eyes had taunting lights in them, warm and inviting. She waited, with no idea what was coming.

'It was the way you kept looking at me when I was working in the chalet. I don't think you realised you were doing it, but you so patently viewed me as some strange mutant, a sort of slug under a stone, a species you'd never come across before. Every time you walked past me you flashed me this same glance—puzzled, distrustful, suspicious. In the end I couldn't stand it a moment longer!'

'I'm sorry, I really am. I didn't mean to be rude. I just couldn't work out——

She stopped. What she hadn't been able to work out was why she felt so compulsively drawn to him, when there was nothing about his life, and therefore, presumably, his character, that appealed to her.

But those feelings she would keep to herself. She did not want him to know how she felt, because she was sure it was not reciprocated. Oh, he found her attractive, she knew that. He even fancied her enough to have kissed her the other night. But that was the sort of thing that happened all the time on skiing holidays, the occasional clinch, the casual affair. While what she felt was almost overwhelming. She longed to touch him, hold him, get as close to him as she possibly could, in every conceivable way. And, if he felt even a fraction of this, then he would not be able to sit so calmly across the table from her. She reached for her glass, and as he did so his fingers circled her wrist.

'Ski with me this afternoon, Sarah?' His voice was low, compulsive. She nodded. 'And have dinner with me tonight?'

Her voice did not seem to work properly. It came out squeaky and high. All the feelings in her body seemed to be concentrated on the point where his fingers touched her bare flesh. 'I'd like that, very much. But what about the others?'

'Others? Oh——' He dismissed them with a dash of his hand. 'They can entertain themselves. I want to celebrate, Sarah! My return to my own life! And I want you to do it with me.'

She looked at his grasp on her slender wrist, the strong fingers, the hand with its fringe of dark hair, and she swallowed. She wanted to, more than anything in the world. But among the excitement beating inside her she felt a wriggle of deep fear.

Today might be wonderful, all that she could want. But what about tomorrow, and the day after, and the day after that? Her life was happy, carefree, wonderfully enjoyable. She cherished it that way. And the hurt she had known before— there was no way she wanted to go through that again.

But, as she looked at the fingers on her wrist, she knew it was already too late. It had been a fragile thing anyway, this life built on work alone, an edifice built on necessity, flimsy as a house of cards. Now James had huffed and puffed at it, and it was about to be blown to the far corners of the mountains.

There was nothing, nothing in this world she could do to stop it happening. It had been a phase in her life, a necessary phase, but one that was now over. She hadn't known it then, but it had been over from that first moment, when she and James had literally run into each other outside her room and the scent of his warm flesh in her nostrils had set her alight with compulsive need.

It was almost like skiing, she thought. She'd been going along, down a nice easy slope in the sunshine, but now she was rushing fast downhill, almost faster than she could cope with. At the bottom would be falls, bruises. The best she could hope for was that her injuries would not be too serious, and she would be able to pick herself up again—older, wiser, maybe even harder than the person she was now.

Slowly she raised her eyes to his, and the long look that went between them set all her pulses hammering.

She swallowed. 'I'd like that. I'd like that very much indeed.'

CHAPTER EIGHT

'ENOUGH?' He raised a dark eyebrow, mouth crooked quizzically.

She bent over her poles, hair hanging down, gasping and laughing. 'I guess so.' She flipped back her head, smiling at him openly, showing him her joy. She had never, in all her years of skiing, enjoyed herself so much.

Until today she had thought that skiing alone was the best thing, but now she knew that skiing with someone who shared her feelings about the mountains was even better.

Over lunch they had pored over the ski map, planning as extensive a route over interconnecting runs and lifts as they could devise, with James swiftly dismissing her view that he should not tax himself.

'I'm going to ache tomorrow, anyway,' he told her. 'I want it to be for a good reason.'

So, fortified by food and wine, they had taken the ski bus to the next valley and spent the afternoon exploring the runs and bars of the neighbouring resort.

There had been little chance to talk, but words had seemed unnecessary. It was extraordinary. It was as if they had known each other for years, for ever. And when they took a chair-lift that allowed them to sit together and James had put his arm round her and hugged her close, squeezing her tight in his exuberance at the afternoon's sport, it had seemed the most natural thing in the world.

Their last run, though, had been demanding. They had taken the lift to the highest point in the valley and from there taken a tortuous route over a ridge and down along some of the most precipitous runs in the area towards their own resort. It was a taxing route at the best of times, but with the sun going, and the snow that had melted in the day's sunshine turning to ice, it had needed maximum concentration to get down safely.

Sarah had started as guide, but James had instinctively taken the lead skiing carefully and well, and always turning to watch her safely down the more treacherous stretches, applauding her with his eyes as she arrived safely and in perfect control beside him.

Before their final descent, they stopped at a bar and took their drinks out on to the terrace to look down on the roofs and buildings of the resort way below them.

The sun was finally setting, brilliant and cold, behind the mountains, dusk was thickening the air and the skiers flashing past below them looked like homing pigeons flocking home to roost.

Neither of them spoke, but the same thing was on both their minds, Sarah could not have said how she knew it, but she was certain.

The day had been magical, a miracle for James, back on skis for the first time in years, and a miracle for her because she had never known such closeness and empathy with anyone before. They had been like eagles, swooping together over the high white peaks alone in the brilliance of sun and snow.

But now they had come back to earth again. The terrace was filling up and shouts and laughter were intruding into their peaceful silence. And the run back down to the village would be about as exhilarating as a journey on a crowded commuter train. She sighed. It had been wonderful, but she was sure that now the best of it was over.

James, who had been lost in his own contemplation of the valley below, looked round, and, when he saw her face he put out a hand and covered hers. It was cool and firm, and his eyes were thoughtful.

There was a tightness in her throat. She wanted to be alone with him. She wanted him to embrace her, to hold her close and kiss her as he had the other evening, but more so, more warmly and intimately than before. A kiss that held all the knowledge of their new closeness.

His mouth moved slightly as he looked at her, as if the very same thought was on his mind.

'What's the matter?

'Nothing. I just hate coming down from the moutains. All these people——'

He played with her fingers, and there was a sadness in his voice. 'Things don't last for ever. It's a lesson I've had to learn. Not even something as good as today.'

His words echoed hollowly in her head. They were a warning to her, clear as a bell, to read nothing too much into their companionship. It was just another ski-slope romance, they said, heady as mountain air one day and finished the next.

She looked at him bleakly. Well, she'd take it for what it was. She was tired of being sensible, of always doing the right thing. She wanted James more than she had ever wanted anyone in her whole life, and if he was hers to have, for however brief a time, then she was going to grasp the offer with both hands.

'We've still got dinner,' he said. 'You're not going to back out on me, are you?'

'No, of course not.'

'Do you know somewhere quiet—where we aren't likely to bump into anyone you know?'

'There's a lot of places the chalet girls don't go to—all the pricey ones! But a lot of them are very pretentious, like the disco we went to the other night.'

He pulled an expressive face.

'My favourite place in town is the Skiers' Bar. Visitors hardly ever find their way there, but the food is rather basic.'

'Who goes there?' he asked keenly.

'The real skiers. Locals, people who live and work here. Instructors and guides.'

He looked thoughtful, dubious.

'Maybe we could have a drink there, before going on somewhere,' she urged. She longed to show him off, dark, handsome James. 'It's not a place many chalet girls go to. You won't be mobbed by giggling females, I promise you.'

Her face was eager, and when he saw her look the doubt went slowly from his eyes. He moved his hand to ruffle her hair and for a second she felt his fingers brush the soft skin of her neck and she shivered deeply and secretly. 'All right. But what about afterwards?'

'There's a place a little way out of town, in an old chalet, that's meant to be superb. I've never been there. I think it really is expensive, but the food is worth it.'

'We'll book a table when we get back.' He started to get up. 'Come on, before we stiffen up too much. Or before I do, I suppose it isn't a problem for you, but I'm going to ache like hell tomorrow, unless I get in a hot bath soon.'

She got up reluctantly. Back at the chalet there would be Brad and Barbara, the superior Kerry and the disruptive Ned. She wanted to stay away from them all, up here, alone, with James. She did not want their leering, knowing assessment of her and James together, the gossip and speculation that would follow, as it had followed from James' long trip yesterday with Kerry.

That thought made her pause as she snapped shut the clasps of her boots.

'James——'

'What?'

She fumbled for words and failed to find them. 'Nothing. It's not important. Not now.'

Nothing lasted for ever. Hadn't he just told her that? Not his dalliance with Kerry, or his involvement with her. There was no point complicating things with unnecessary demands and explanations.

Even so, as she followed his lithe figure down the final slope to the chalet, she felt consumed with a jealousy that frightened her. Never in all her life had she felt so passionately possessive about another person, and the intensity of the feeling shook her so much that she faltered and almost fell on the gentle slope.

She was unutterably relieved to find the chalet deserted. She was still shaking from the wave of emotion that had swept over her, and knew she would have found it impossible to put on her cheerful chalet girl face and cope with shouted demands for tea or a drink.

James went straight to his room and so did she. She stripped off her skiing clothes and put on her

Japanese robe. In the mirror a stranger's face greeted her. Her face was tanned from the day's sun, her eyes were bright with emotion. But there was a new, apprehensive depth in them that had not been there before, a set seriousness to her mouth that hinted at future pain.

It was the face of a woman falling in love, she thought, a face that was vulnerable to uncontrollable pleasure and unimaginable pain, and she turned quickly away because she had forgotten how it was to feel this way—if she had ever really felt it before.

The bath, she thought practically. James must have a bath before his muscles seized up completely. She crossed the hallway and sluiced hot water into the huge white tub, pouring in a generous amount of bath gel for good measure. As she bent down to swirl them around James came through the door.

'After you—I'll have the same water.'

She straightened, her face flushed and damp.

'It's for you.'

James was wearing nothing but a towel, stretched tight over hips. The powerful muscles she had seen at work all day now gleamed among the steam. His shoulders were broad and firm, his thighs strongly muscled. There was a scatter of dark hair across his chest, dipping in an arrowing line to the edge of the white towel.

'But you must need one.'

'I'll have it afterwards—I'll have your water.'

'I can wait.'

'No, you need it more than me.'

It was ridiculous, like a squabble between schoolchildren. Yours. No, yours.

James grinned. 'There's a simple solution.' He angled his head at the bath. 'It's big enough for two.'

Instantly through her mind whirled a million images: water and white bubbles; silken skin and wet hair, lips, teeth, hands, closeness and desire. She hesitated.

He read her eyes. 'I'd love to,' he said softly. 'But we mustn't. No.' He walked to her through the steam and took her by the shoulders, gently. She could smell his damp skin and it made her body tense with longing beneath her robe. Then he kissed her, long, slow and carefully, taking her lips with a tenderness that made her hands spread wide on his naked back, wanting to encompass all of him and hold him close.

His breath rasped in his throat when he drew back, and his eyes had darkened. He pushed her hair back from her face, restlessly. 'My little skier,' he said, shakily. 'I don't want to let you go.'

She scoured his face, wanting to imprint every detail on her memory. She saw the faint lines at the corners of his eyes, the dark shadow of his beard, the thickness of his hair, carelessly tousled. Her hands were still holding his arms and the flesh was warm and firm.

'I don't want you to,' she confessed, her eyes lifted to his.

Now it was his turn to hesitate. His hands were on her waist and he ran them up the sides of her body, under her arms, feeling her slender ribcage beneath her robe. She knew he wanted to touch her closer, more intimately, and she shivered, anticipating his touch on the aching softness of her breasts.

Behind her the noise of the running water changed pitch, splashing in a furious cascade.

'Oh, God!' James dropped his hold and sprang forward, turning off the taps as water foamed in a waterfall out of the brimming bath.

She turned, dazed, focusing only slowly on the problem.

'Is there a mop, or a cloth?'

'Yes, here.'

She knelt in the water and opened a cupboard, getting out cloths and buckets. Together they began to tackle the problem, oblivious of a shadow that darkened the open doorway.

'I say, Kerry,' drawled Ned. 'Come and look at this little scene. Touching, isn't it? Such domesticity.'

Sarah looked up and met Ned's jeering eyes. Then Kerry was beside him and her eyes were only for James' half-naked figure. When they tore themselves away they went straight to Sarah, flashing a simple messege—I want him, you leave him alone!

She had no idea what her expression said to Kerry in reply, but she knew her thoughts were every bit as savage. You aren't going to have him, she vowed silently, because he's mine! And then, because she was honest, and because she knew the skiing scene well enough to know the real score, she added to herself with bitter sadness, at least for the time being.

James barely glanced up, but continued methodically to mop up.

'If you're staying,' he told them, 'you could lend a hand, instead of just propping up the doorway.'

'We were just discussing where to eat tonight,' said Ned, 'since Sarah's been let off duty.' His voice twisted sarcastically as he spoke her name, and he pulled a face at her, as if to remind her who was the real cook about the place.

She tried to ignore him, but her heart skipped a beat as the memory of her elaborate deception of James and all his guests came back to her.

'That's your problem. I'm taking Sarah out

to dinner.'

'Sarah?' Kerry's voice was waspish. 'But I thought we discussed going to Les Halles again tonight.'

'We did—discuss it. But that's not the same as deciding to go there.' James stopped his work and looked up coldly. 'And anyway, I rather expected you would be tied up at the hospital today, sitting by Tim's bed.'

'I rang, but they said he was comfortable. There's nothing I can do, and it's too far to go every day.' Kerry pouted.

'Every day till tomorrow, when he's being flown home?' James' tone was contemptuous. He watched, expressionless, as Kerry turned and left, then his gaze went to Ned. 'You want to help?' He proffered his younger brother a cloth.

Ned shook his head insolently. 'Not me. I've done enough chores around the place this past week, you ask Sarah.' He looked pointedly at her, then back at James and the chaotic intimacy of the steamy bathroom. 'Oh, and James,' he added, as he made his departure, 'if you're really serious about buying out NewSki I should take a close look at their staffing policies.' He paused dramatically. 'Their chalet girls, for example, aren't at all what they seem.'

CHAPTER NINE

THINGS that evening went badly from the first.

Sarah looked miserably round the Skiers' Bar and wondered how their warmth and closeness could have been so completely shattered.

It was all Ned's fault, she thought savagely. Once James was safely ensconced in the bath she had gone in search of him, only to find he, too, was soaking in the tub.

'I want to talk to you!' she hissed, through the locked door.

'All in good time, my sweet. I'm making myself beautiful for you,' he carolled back.

'Well, you can save yourself the bother!'

She had flung back to her own room, anxious not to bump into Kerry on top of her other problems, and dropped back on the bed. After a time there was a knock on the door and her heart had leapt up. James! She jumped to her feet. 'Come in.'

'I thought you'd never ask.' Ned barged in, in his bathrobe, his hair still wet from the bath.

'What are you doing?'

'I thought you wanted to talk to me.'

'I do, but not like this!'

Ned's eyes were mocking. 'How then, like this?' With agility, he bounced on to her bed, pulling her by the wrist so she landed with him.

She struggled up. 'For goodness' sake, stop it!'

She looked round. Her door was wide open. Any moment James might come out of the bathroom and

131

see them, yet Ned was lacing his fingers comfortably behind his head and making it plain he planned to stay. She pushed the door closed, then leaned against it.

'Why did you say those things earlier—about chalet girls? What were you playing at? I thought I could trust you!'

'Aha.' He wagged a finger at her. 'Never trust anyone except yourself. That's what my dear departed father always used to say. It's all perfectly simple, Sarah. You see, I expected a little more—shall we say, gratitude?—for the way I've helped you out. It's been a bit of a busman's holiday for me, so far, having to think up all these menus and shopping lists. I thought there might be some mileage in it, for me, by the end of the fortnight.'

'You mean, you thought I'd go to bed with you,' she said bluntly.

Before today she would have used all her management skills to sweet-talk her way out of the situation, sending Ned on his way with joking laughter covering her rejection of him. But now, after today with James, she had no time for such wiles. 'Well, you thought wrong. I don't pay for favours in that way.'

His expression hardened. 'I should get off your high horse, Sarah dear. It doesn't become you. Not after what we saw earlier.'

'And what was that—two people mopping up a bathroom floor? Very damning!'

'The vibrations in that room were as steamy as the atmosphere. Anyone could tell you and Big Brother were on the brink of hopping in the tub together. I don't suppose you expected anyone back quite so soon.'

'Well, you're wrong about that. I ran a bath for

James because he'd been skiing and he knew he'd be stiff in the morning. We were,' she hesitated, 'talking and didn't notice the water.'

His mouth was open and he hadn't noticed her stumbling explanation.

'What did you say? James! Skiing! He doesn't ski.'

'He does. He skies superbly. I should know, we've been right over to the next valley today. He told me about his accident, and how he hasn't skied for years because of it, but now he's decided to start again.'

'Well, well, well,' Ned said softly and slowly. 'This is a turn-up. He told you about that—all about it?'

She shrugged. 'Enough. He said he used to ski a lot, but after his leg was pinned he decided to give it up.'

'And that's all?'

'More or less.' She frowned. 'Why?'

Ned swung his legs down. 'Oh, there's more. Plenty more. And no doubt Brother James will tell you when he judges the moment ripe.'

'What do you mean?' He was sowing all manner of doubts and uncertainties in her mind. Her eyes watched him warily as he came towards her.

'I mean, Little Miss Chalet Girl,' he said cruelly. 'I'm sure he'll tell you everything if he decides to really turn you on. And if he does—I guarantee it won't be those sheets you're between tonight!' His finger stabbed towards her bed. In his voice was all the deep-held resentment of a younger brother who had lived his entire life in the shadow of an older rival.

'Of course,' he continued reflectively, 'if he plays his trump card, I could always play mine. And that would be a real spanner in the works, wouldn't it?

I don't suppose he'd take too kindly to having the wool pulled over his eyes about your cooking prowess. Not when thinks back to all those compliments he's thrown your way. Remember the cheese soufflé? The *crème brûlée*?'

As he spoke he was coming towards her, pulling her to him. Her mind was so busy trying to puzzle out his torrent of hints and threats that he had pinned his arms about her before she fully realised what his intentions were.

Then his lips were seeking hers, thin and horribly soft. She turned her head, struggling, but he was too strong for her. In their tussle they stumbled against the door and it clicked from the latch and swung open. Outside James was crossing from the bathroom towards his own door. When he saw their entwined figures he stopped, stock still.

She raised her head, her lips reddened and her hair in disarray, and met his startled and disbelieving gaze. Then Ned spoke, to all intents and purposes oblivious to James' presence, 'My God, Sarah,' he breathed loudly, 'you really know how to get me going. Don't be too late tonight. I'll wait for you in my room as usual, after everyone's asleep.'

Now, three hours later, she looked desperately round the bar. James, beside her, had retreated firmly back into his cold, controlled self.

'Is it Ned?' she asked him, desperate to break through the barriers that seemed to divide them. 'Is it what you thought you saw earlier? You must believe me, what I told you. There's nothing going on between us.'

His anger had been so obvious, she had half expected him to cancel their evening together. He had not done so, but ever since they'd left the chalet he had been barely civil to her.

Now he turned his head to her. 'I want to believe that, Sarah. I really do. I mean, I can't imagine what any woman would see in such a half-baked creature as my younger brother. But at the same time I can't ignore the evidence of my own eyes. Every time I turn round I find you and him tangled up together. You say it's an accident—but how many times can you possibly have the self-same accident without it becoming rather more than coincidental?'

'Ned came to my room to speak to me,' she said tightly. Her hands were clenched balls in her lap. 'I told him to go away. He didn't. He grabbed me and kissed me. And what he said—that was just for your benefit. I didn't want him to touch me. If you must know, it made me feel ill!'

'Good old Ned,' he said sarcastically. 'Always one for the subtle approach. But what interests me is what on earth he had to speak to you about that was so urgent? Was it the same thing he was dropping hints about earlier—all that cloak and dagger stuff about chalet girls? Perhaps you'd like to explain all that to me, Sarah? Then we might begin to make some sense of this ridiculous muddle.'

'I can't!' She turned hard round in her seat to face him, pleading with her eyes. 'James, it's all just—something silly. It isn't a bit important——'

'So it won't matter if you tell me.'

'It's not that simple,' she said, with anguish. 'Not while——' She stopped. She did not want to get on to the dangerous ground of his bid for NewSki. Better to pretend that the beginning of Ned's pointed remark had been drowned out for her by the splashing of the bath water. 'I can tell you later. I will tell you, but please, not now.'

He sighed, and returned to his perusal of the bar. She couldn't be sure, but she sensed that on top of being angry with her he was also on edge, alert and unrelaxed.

Well, that made two of them. She had had such high hopes of this evening, had dressed with such care in her best black sheath dress. When they'd left the chalet together her heart had been knocking like a teenager's.

But now his eyes were flickering restlessly around the room, while she perched on the very edge of her stool, her knuckles showing white in her lap.

'Perhaps there are questions I'd like to ask you,' she burst out in her misery. Her voice sounded petulant and she hated the tenor of it. 'Like why it took you and Kerry half the night to visit Tim in hospital?'

His eyes went back to her, dark as pits, and his voice was cold and smooth. 'Because we had dinner, and then we went on to a late-night bar. It was all Kerry's idea, I can assure you. She doesn't much care to be without an escort.'

'It's obscene—with Tim lying in hospital like that!'

His eyes warmed for the first time that evening, smile lines webbing their corners. 'Not nearly as obscene as she would have liked it to be.'

'You mean——'

'I mean she made me a very explicit proposal about how she would like to spend the rest of the night. Admittedly it was after rather a lot of wine and best brandy, but even so, I've rarely heard such plain speaking from female lips!'

Her eyes examined his. 'And you——'

'Kerry is a very compelling women,' he said. 'Her attractions are obvious. I'll admit I was tempted for a moment. But I was also angry with her for tempting me like that. As you rightly say, it was obscene. I think she realised how I felt after I'd finished replying to her.'

'She fancies you like crazy. I saw how she looked at you tonight, when she saw us in the bathroom together.'

He inclined his head. 'It's not particularly flattering. She's the kind of woman who abhors a vacuum—with Tim out of circulation she automatically looks for a replacement escort. I'm sure the next one down her list is Ned.'

She pulled a face. 'I'm sure she'll be lucky there. I think she already has been.'

He slanted a look at her. 'And you mind?'

'Of course I don't mind! Not in the way you mean! I just find it all rather—revolting.'

'Oh?'

'There's something about skiing—I don't know if it's the mountain air, or all that exercise, or the alcohol, or what—but half the people who come here seem to end up behaving like animals. It's what we were talking about the other night, at the hospital.

'One group I was with once seemed to swap partners every night. It was a big joke at first, but by the end of the fortnight two of the men were hurling bottles at each other's heads. Then there was another couple who just sort of launched themselves at each other one night in the middle of the main room. We kept thinking they'd stop, or at least retire into privacy somewhere, but they didn't——'

She suddenly laughed, remembering the absurdity of the scene, and James looked at her face and smiled. 'What happened?'

'All the talking sort of died away, and people just

stared and stared with a horrible fascination. It was very late at night, we'd all been to a party, and I suppose we were all the wrong side of sober, so nothing seemed quite real.

'Someone poured a bottle of Perrier water over the man, which rather damped his ardour, at least enough for their friends to drag them away. In the morning she was very shame-faced, although he didn't seem to care very much.'

She stared into her glass and thought about that night and all the other chalet party evenings she had known, a long whirl of smoky rooms, changing faces, glasses emptying and filling, and she felt suddenly sad and achingly lonely.

'I thought chalet girls did the job for the nightlife as much as anything.'

'Some do, but others become jaded when they realise there's no point in getting tipsy because it makes it impossible to work the next day, and there's no point getting involved with anyone because they just pack their bags and go . . .' Her voice tailed away. She didn't want to think about bags being packed, people leaving.

'So, no involvements—since your big break-up?' James quizzed her casually but pointedly.

'None. What about you?' she ventured cautiously. 'Ned told me he was a last-minute standby because your girlfriend wasn't coming.' Even as the words were out she cursed herself for mentioning Ned's name again, but James only grinned, a little wryly.

'I have to own up to a rather——' he hesitated, selecting his words carefully, 'footloose life when I was younger. Later on, when my businesses started to prosper, I decided I ought to think about settling down. Charlotte was totally suitable in every way. There was only one slight problem.' There was a roughness in his voice that drew her gaze to him. His eyes, warmer now and lingering over her face, made her shiver inside. 'I didn't manage to fall in love with her. I called the whole thing off just before I came here.'

'You certainly didn't seem particularly happy when you arrived,' she said tentatively.

'Happy? It was one of the most wretched weeks of my life! There I was, stuck in a chalet with all these people I didn't care a lot for, with only work and gloomy thoughts for company. It isn't very nice to hurt someone you care for, even if it's for the best. I barely felt alive until I put myself back on skis today.'

'I don't understand how you could have not skied for so long—you're fantastic, as good as the professionals. Why, you're every bit as good as Claude here!'

She waved her hand emphatically towards the doorway where Claude Montaine stood shrugging off his coat, and her heart lifted. She wanted to show James off to Claude. She wanted James to meet Claude. She was sure the two men would hit it off.

'Claude!' She called a greeting, turning back to James. 'I'd love you to meet him. He's a marvellous man.'

But James had already stood up and put down coins on the table.

'I don't feel much like socialising tonight,' he said shortly. 'I'd rather we left.'

'Just hello,' she protested, but James was already pulling on his jacket, turning away. 'The table's booked for nine,' he said shortly. 'I'll see you outside in a moment.'

'James——'

She stared disbelievingly at his back. By the time Claude had answered her summoning wave and come to the table. James was out of sight. His departure was abrupt to the point of rudeness, yet James was not a rude man. She didn't understand it. She felt she did not understand anything about him, and Ned's mysterious words about his brother's hidden past came to perplex and disturb her.

'Sarah, *bonsoir*,' Claude kissed her roundly on both cheeks, but his eyes were elsewhere. 'Who is this man you are always with? This mysterious stranger? What does he say his name is?'

'His name's James Holloway. He's part of my chalet group. Claude, he's a brilliant skier. We had the most fantastic day out today!'

'Holloway,' Claude repeated.

'That's right. Holloway.' She thought he was worried about his pronunciation.

'Are you sure?'

'Of course I'm sure.' She laughed, exasperated. 'Claude, what is this?'

Claude stared at the empty doorway as if it would provide answers to the questions that ran through his mind.

''ow good a skier?' He quizzed, intently, his French accent heavy in his emotion.

She shook her head. 'I don't know—very good. First class.'

'As good as me?'

'I'm not sure. He's out of practice, but I guess so, Claude——'

'Mmm.' Claude tapped a cigarette from a crumpled pack and lit it reflectively. 'Out of practice, you say? Well, I don't think that's James Holloway at all. You ask him. If he tells you the truth I think you'll find out he's someone very different. You ask him—you ask him from me. And if he tells you the whole story, then tell him Claude says welcome back.'

She didn't, though. Instead she went to the cloakroom and stood shakily in front of the mirror, biting her lip.

The mirror, which was old and stained with rust, showed her a patchy reflection. She still looked lovely. She had put on a silver choker and earrings, and her face was luminous with youth and health. Her eyes and teeth were dazzling white against her light tan and sun-streaked hair, which was caught up in a bow of black lace.

But there was worry in her blue eyes and a line of tension between her brows. She pushed her hands up under her hair and pulled it back from her face, hoping the pain of her tugging fingers would concentrate her spinning thoughts.

James said he didn't ski. Then he did, like an angel. Ned said he hadn't told her the half about himself, and Claude seemed to think he was someone quite different. She didn't understand anything any more, least of all her own place in the tangled web.

It made her feel young and vulnerable, a foolish girl, in love for the first time.

But she wasn't foolish. She tipped her chin in the mirror. She was Sarah Milner, with her fair share of brains and beauty, a fistful of qualifications, a senior job, and an ever-growing knowledge of the world.

She glared hard at her reflection. What about James? she thought, with a sudden spurt of anger.

What did James have to say about all this mystery?

Nothing, so far, but all that was going to have to change! And anger stilled her shaking hands and gave her the resolve to carry her out of the door and up the steps to the street.

It was completely deserted. Snow was beginning to fall again, tiny flakes spinning around and around in the streetlamps. The icy chill struck the flush from her cheeks. She hesitated, looked this way, then that. The cold made her pull her coat tighter about her.

Surely he couldn't have just gone—or could he? She felt she didn't know anything any more.

But the thought struck her with such a desperate desolation that she knew she didn't care who he was, or why he had shrouded himself with such mystery and deception. It was a sharp pain in her heart, and the only thing that mattered was that he shouldn't have gone, shouldn't have left her alone, without him.

Then there was a movement across the street. Part of the black shadows stirred and stepped forward and it was James, as dark a figure as always, dark hair, dark jacket, dark trousers. Only his profile was lit, strong and sensuous in the shadow of the streetlight.

Without thought she ran towards him, across the street. He came forward, too. And although she had meant to be cold and angry, had meant to say, Who are you? What's going on? I have to know, she didn't. She didn't need to know anything. Only that he was here, waiting for her, and that those were his arms going around her, catching her to him, holding her close, and those were his eyes, dark, tender, on her face, and his lips seeking hers, cold mouth against cold mouth, hot breath entwining, lips moving as they strove to be closer still, seeking, wanting, finding, knowing.

CHAPTER TEN

WHO knew how long they stood there? Although when they finally moved apart there was a fine white dusting of snow on their coats.

She had felt shaky before. Now her knees felt almost too weak to hold her up. She bent her neck and let her forehead rest lightly against his chest while she recovered, and she felt his hand caress her hair.

'OK?' His voice was low, gentle.

She nodded, although she wasn't. She had never been kissed like that before, never in her life. There had been worlds, continents, in their embrace, such tenderness and pent-up passion. Such confusion mixed with such utter certainty.

She wondered what he would say. If he suggested abandoning the meal, going back to the chalet, then she would follow him willingly.

But he took her arm and began to walk her slowly along the street towards the square where the taxis waited.

The silence between them was eloquent. They both knew that the smallest sentence would release an avalanche of words, and they rode in continuing silence up the winding hill, past fairy-tale Alpine chalets to the restaurant.

Once there she fled to the cloakroom to brush her hair and repair her lipstick, but the actions did little to repair her composure. Her eyes were too bright, her lips parted with nervous expectation. She looked almost feverish, she thought, and patted cold water against her cheeks to try and calm herself.

James sat at the table and watched her walk back towards him with open appreciation.

'Well?' he said eventually, and then he laughed, deeply and freely, and he was again the man she had spent the day with, carefree and sure of himself, and she knew that, whatever his secret was, it could not be so terrible after all.

'Who are you?' She was smiling at his laughter, shaking her head. 'What's all this about? Everyone seems to know but me.'

'What did Claude say?'

'You know him! He seems to think he knows you.'

'Not that well. We were rivals some years back.'

'Rivals? In love?'

'No. Not in love. In skiing. Speed skiing.'

'Oh!' Her mouth was wide with surprise as the fragments of confusion began to fall into some shadowy semblance of order. 'So that's why you're so good——'

'Proficient, no longer that good,' he put in. 'Apart from being out of practice, I realised today I've lost my taste for taking risks. Life and health now seem far more important than the glittering prizes.'

'Claude said you weren't James Holloway.'

'Holloway is my name. But I raced under my mother's name, Jensen. At nineteen I thought it sounded better!'

'James Jensen! Oh, of course! Why didn't I—I remember watching you on television when I was at school.' Every Sunday afternoon she had sat breathless before the small screen in the sixth-form common-room, wondering how the racers found the nerve and muscle to fling themselves down the mountains in the way that they did.

'Thanks. That makes me feel as ancient as a silent movie star.'

'It was only seven years ago. You always wore black, black helmet and everything. Oh, and I remember you falling.' She shut her eyes and saw the terrible accident again, the figure swerving too steeply, losing control and falling, spinning, tumbling to a dreadful stop against the crash barrier. The commentator hadn't known what to say because he was sure it had been a fatal accident. Only later in the programme did he give the news that Britain's James Jensen was critical, and being flown out to hospital.

'My swansong,' said James, pouring wine, and she noticed a pulse of tension at the corner of his jaw as he remembered the day. 'It was in Austria, on the Hannenkahm. I was twenty-five and everyone predicted I'd be right at the top next season. Then it was all wiped out at a stroke.

'I spent the next six months in hospitals of various kinds. The outside was hardly touched, the only scars I've got are on one leg, but the inside was thoroughly mangled. My left leg was broken in five separate places, and none of them clean fractures. At one time they thought I wouldn't walk again. Then they thought that leg would always be slightly shorter.'

'But you haven't even got a limp.'

'No, I made damn sure of that. I exercised every single day, stretching and strengthening the muscles. I think I had some fool notion that if I tried hard enough I might even be able to take up where I'd left off. I was daft enough to think I could somehow make a comeback and grab those trophies that had nearly been in my grasp before. When they told me I had no hope in hell of ever racing again, I went into a black depression.'

He looked at her and she waited. Somehow she was sure he had barely spoken to anyone of this before.

'It's hard to imagine if you've never lived that sort of life, but downhill racing was everything to me. Ever since I first skied, as a schoolboy, I'd lived for nothing else. I followed the snow all over the world—Canada, America, Australia. I washed dishes in skiing resorts, worked as an instructor, fought for sponsorship.

'Finally it all began to happen. I was on the circuit, recognised as a serious competitor. I began to climb the league tables, people began to notice me.'

Still she waited, quiet, listening. His eyes were on hers.

'It was a great life for someone like me, young, no ties. I was a big fish in a small pond, heads turned when I entered the room. There were parties, and more parties, and ski groupies——' His mouth crooked at her, almost warily. 'As you so rightly said earlier, the mountain air seems to go to people's heads. I enjoyed all that, and I'd be a liar if I said otherwise, although by the end it was beginning to pall.

'But the only thing that really mattered to me was the racing, pushing myself to the edge, the absolute limit, living on adrenalin. I loved everything about it, the technical side, working out how to get the best out of the equipment, the most out of an angle of a slope, the moment before you pushed off, when you felt that prickle of fear.'

She had never heard him speak so much. Even around the dinner-table at the chalet, his contributions had been short comments or isolation stories. And she had never heard him speak of himself before. Although his voice was measured and sure, she was certain such personal revelations were a rare glimpse into a deeply private personality, and her eyes did not leave his as he talked.

'So can you imagine how I felt when they took it all away from me? I felt I might as well have been in a wheelchair for life. Even dead, because there was nothing left I wanted to live for.'

She drew in her breath sharply.

'Surely not——'

He shrugged slightly. 'It seems crazy now, but that was how I was. I refused to see my skiing friends, shut myself away from everything I'd known. I was full of anger, looking for someone to blame.'

His eyes blazed darkly, and she could see he was seeing again some vision from the past.

'What happened? You're not like that now.'

'I was still in a convalescent home at the time—surrounded by people who'd had motorbike accidents or fallen off ladders; you can imagine what a cheerful bunch we were. There was a doctor there who thought it would help me to see a video of the television programme that showed my accident. I didn't want to, I remember telling him very firmly what he could do with it!' His eyes crinkled. 'But he insisted. We watched it together, and he made me talk him through it and explain to him exactly what had gone wrong.

'For the very first time I began to see, and accept that it had been entirely my fault, I'd pushed too hard, cut a turn too fine, not taken full account of the ice . . . That was the best thing possible for me. It made me take responsibility for myself again. I discharged myself within the week and by the end of the year I'd managed to throw myself into a new career.' He swallowed down his wine. 'I can't say that marketing meetings and annual reports have ever given me quite the thrill of going at eighty miles an hour down the Lauberhorn, but there's some excitement to be had from building up a business from nothing.'

She played with the stem of her glass, eyes down now on the table, struck with feelings for the young man who'd had to go through so much pain and bitter loss.

That man wasn't James, the man sitting across the table from her, she could see that. There was a maturity about him, a self-knowledge, that must only have come at great personal expense.

She looked up. 'Why did you change your name?'

'I suppose it was symbolic, James Jensen had been a downhill racer. He didn't exist any more. I wanted to bury him for good.'

'Oh, I see.'

'And there was something else, Sarah.' The sound of her name made her look up, meeting his eyes again.

'I mentioned the parties——'

She nodded, fighting back the instant jealous hatred of all the girls he had known and loved.

'Well, I discovered that one of the very few good things to come out of the whole débâcle was being able to return to anonymity. It's marvellous to be the star of the show when you're twenty-three and very full of yourself, but slowly you come to realise that no one sees you for what you really are. There might be girls throwing themselves at you from every direction, but it's only because of your name, your fame. They just want to boast of knowing you.

'And the others, the ones who aren't like that, are the ones who hang back and you never get to meet. As James Holloway, at least I knew I was getting a genuine response from people I met.'

'But surely people remembered, I mean Claude——'

He shook his head. 'Most people have very short memories, and racers don't have particularly famous faces because they're always muffled up in their equipment. Anyway the racing world is tiny, and although my business is in sports equipment, not much has been directly to do with skiing so far. And I've never been near a European skiing resort till now. So if it hadn't been for Claude Montaine, I might just have got away with it altogether.'

'Wouldn't you have even told me?' she asked him, pained to think it was only Claude's chance intervention that had caused the truth to come spilling out. 'After today, on the mountains, when we had such fun together!' Her voice sounded young, eager, anguished.

He took her hand, splaying her fingers on his palm, stroking her skin with his thumb.

'I didn't want to.'

'Oh.' There was bitter disappointment in her voice.

'Don't look like that. It wasn't that I wanted to deceive you.' He sighed and his eyes caressed her. 'This is very difficult to say. It's just that whatever is going on between us . . .' He stopped, then went on, bluntly, 'You're a chalet girl, Sarah. You're crazy about skiing. I felt that if you knew who I was, or rather had been, it would inevitably colour your judgement of me.'

She looked at him, remembering Ned's bitter and jealous words about James's 'trump card'. And his predicted outcome from the disclosure. She blushed.

'You mean I'd be like one of your ski groupies! If you think that, then you obviously don't know me at all!' Although how could he, she thought, honestly, when she had taken such trouble to mask herself from him?

'Oh, Sarah, Sarah,' she mourned. He looked at her hurt eyes and bright cheeks, and his look was like a caress. 'I don't think that. I think you're bright and beautiful and warm and resourceful.' He smiled, white teeth showing between firm lips. 'Shall I go on? I could—all evening.' His fingers tightened round her hand. 'You've lit up my life ever since I first saw you. You got me back on skis again, for which I'll be eternally grateful, and at this very moment I'm having the greatest difficulty keeping my hands off you long enough to eat a meal.' He sighed again. 'Maybe it's just my arrogance, but I wanted to be sure. I didn't want to spoil anything by dragging up my past——'

'It's not very flattering to be treated like a school-girl with a crush,' she got out. But perhaps, said a niggling voice of honesty, that's what you are. The feelings she had for James were no means cooled by his revelations.

She studied him covertly under her lashes. It all made sense. It made him whole, not jumbled parts of a picture that did not add up. It explained the strange certainty she had had that he was a man in exile, and it explained more fully the powerful attraction she had felt for him from the first.

She longed for his arms round her, his lips finding hers again, and that longing was only intensified by knowing who he was.

But was that because of his famous name? The glamour and excitement he must have known? Or was it something else?' The knowledge of what had shaped him into the man he was today, his struggles and triumphs and pain?

She hoped it was the latter, felt sure it was. And yet—she understood James' caution.

'Does anyone else at the chalet know?'

He grinned, rather harshly. 'I don't think Tim and Kerry are very interested in anyone but themselves. Brad might have a notion, but he keeps his own counsel. Ned knows, of course. He always resented James Jensen, and all the attention he got. I'm afraid he took a great deal of malicious pleasure in the way he was cut off in his prime.'

'But he would have been so young, just a teenager. It must have been hard for him to live in your shadow.'

His eyes scoured her intently, their grey-blue turning to pure-grey. After a moment he said, 'You always have a good word for Ned, an excuse for his behaviour. I wish I understood what's going on between you two.'

She shook her head vehemently. 'Don't be ridiculous.' But a guilty flush spread across her cheeks and she knew he saw it. She saw him draw breath, hesitate, then decide not to pursue the matter. Even so, a beat of tension marked his cheek and she knew he was angry.

'James——' She leant forward. She urgently wanted to tell him everything. Clear the table of all lies and deception. Then she remembered. It wasn't James Jensen, the skier, she was talking to. It was James Holloway, the businessman, James Holloway who had a bid in for NewSki. And back in the London office of NewSki were Brian and Gail, no doubt biting their nails over the deal, desperate to buy themselves free. Gail, who had persuaded Brian to take her on despite her youth and inexperience, and Brian, who had given her every chance to develop her talents and potential.

She owed them something for their faith in her, their willingness to take her on blind trust, and that something was silence.

He looked at her oddly, waiting for more words to come, but she sighed and leaned back, shaking her head. 'Nothing. It's not important.' He held her eyes for a long moment, but then dropped his gaze to the menu.

'I'm starving,' he said shortly.

She watched him as he ate steadily through the courses. The bad moment passed, and they were soon talking easily, the conversation ranging readily from one subject to the next.

But she could not eat. The dishes set before her were tempting, yet she was too excited, too strung out, to do them justice. Her fork pushed the food aimlessly around her plate while her eyes feasted on James's face and her ears devoured the sound of his voice.

She watched his eyes, and the way their colour changed endlessly as he laughed, or spoke, or looked at her, the fall of his hair, the decisive movements of his hands.

She saw things about him that she had never noticed in anyone else before. The shape of his head made her long to mould it with her hands, and she wanted to touch the skin at his throat with her lips.

Embarassed by the vividness of her thoughts, she

drank more wine and her head spun and the longings came back, three and four times as strong. It was as if the very air vibrated with them because suddenly James' sentence tailed away, and his eyes were on hers with a new intensity, and she saw his lips part slightly to take breath, showing the white, even edge of his teeth.

'Let's go,' he said abruptly, even though their coffee was untouched, and he turned and snapped his fingers for the bill.

Outside the restaurant the snow was still coming down steadily in tiny flakes, like falling dust. He took her hand in his as the door shut behind them and the warmth and colour of the restaurant was replaced by the dark, cold silence of the night.

That simple act was the most powerful touch she had ever known. Her hand felt small in his firm grasp, and she suddenly knew what it would feel like to be loved, protected, cared for. The warmth of skin against skin made her breath catch in her throat. She stopped, turned, and he turned with her and their lips met hungrily, almost angrily, in an urgency that sent her blood pounding fiercely through her veins.

'Damn these jackets,' James said against her lips as he wrestled against their bulk. With one hand he unzipped his jacket and she reached with her arms inside, feeling the warm lines of his body, holding him close to her, lifting her lips again to him to be kissed until her head reeled, and she knew it was the same for him because his body was hard with a desire that he did not bother to hide from her.

But the night air was freezing, and the snow seemed to find its way on to every bare centimetre of skin.

'We didn't ring for a taxi,' she said as he

reluctantly let her go.

'We can walk,' he said. 'It's only about fifteen minutes back to the square, and we can pick up a taxi to the chalet. Unless you're too tired?'

He looked at her assessingly as she shook her head. 'Only I think I need a cooling off period if I'm to behave like a gentleman.'

He took her arm and they set off together into the night. It was a beautiful walk, with the snow falling silently and the mountains unseen, but sentinel, all around. Yet she could not help but feel cast down.

The very last thing in the world that she wanted, she realised, was for James to behave like a gentleman. Her longings were heading in a quite different direction.

CHAPTER ELEVEN

THEY stood together in the hallway and listened. The chalet seemed deserted.

She did not know what would happen now. The long walk back down the mountain road to the resort had been almost magical, their near silence so easy and close it was as if they had been together for years.

But now reality had returned again. They were no longer out there in the white, silent night, two dark figures crunching together over the hard-packed snow, but were back home again, standing among the litter of skis and poles and boots that cluttered the lobby by the front door.

James dropped her arm and she snapped a switch so that violent yellow light poured down on them. It threw harsh shadows on to his face and made him look severe and gaunt. She sensed a tension in him, could feel his thoughts flicking rapidly, while hers seemed stunned by the emotions of the evening.

She dared not examine them closely because she knew too well what she would find there when she did. The word had formed in her mind as they paced down through the night, and her boots had drummed a dull tattoo of it on the road.

It had four letters and began with 'l', but she would not shape it in her mind because it was too big, too frightening an emotion to cope with.

Once before she had thought she had loved, and it had brought her only trouble and pain. Yet what she felt now was a hundred times stronger, a million times more vivid. And that could only mean that the level of hurt would be equally great when James turned his back on her and left.

She turned away and began to unzip her jacket. The warmth of the chalet made her nose begin to run, and she sniffed unromantically until she could find a tissue in her pocket.

James said, 'You need a brandy to warm you up,' and she nodded with relief. A brandy would mean deferring whatever was to happen next, and that suited her just fine, because she neither knew what she wanted, or what he had in mind.

He led the way up the stairs and stirred the fire to life. As he straightened up, she was standing behind him, and he took her quickly and unexpectedly into his arms, then kissed her lightly before dropping his arms and moving to pour them both a drink.

The embrace left her wordless. It had been a touch like the feeling of his hand taking hers outside the restaurant. A caress of certainty and possession, a lover's touch, full of tenderness and passion. Her eyes scarcely left him as he came back through the shadowed room towards her.

Neither of them moved to turn on a lamp.

He peeled off his jacket. 'I take back what I said about warming up. This room is like an oven.'

When he spoke she realised the prickling sensation on her skin was not only to do with his proximity, but with the heat of the fire on her dress.

He had pulled off his tie and loosened the neck of his shirt.

'You must be hot.' He nodded at her wool dress. She looked at him doubtfully and he suddenly grinned, boyish and amused. 'That wasn't a line, Sarah. Just an observation.'

She smiled back at him. 'I'll go and change. It's stifling.'

She returned in her kimono, knowing it flattered her slim figure. It was her robe, but she also often wore it at breakfast time. It was perfectly decent, provided the neck was well closed and the waist securely belted. At least, that was what she told herself, but there was a provocative element in her choice which James registered instantly with his eyes when she came back into the room.

He had settled on the rug by the fire, his back against a chair, and he put up a hand to draw her to him. She knelt down near him and his fingers pushed up under the wide sleeve, stroking the soft skin of her elbow and arm.

'Suppose,' he said huskily, 'it *had* been a line?'

In answer, although he had not known she was going to do it, she leant forward until her lips found his and kissed him. When her eyes opened again she saw he was watching her closely through half lowered lids. He swallowed and drew her down to him and she turned and curled beside him, warm in the crook of his embracing arm.

'I would have fallen for it,' she said willingly. 'You know that.'

He stroked her arm, and for several moments neither of them spoke as they watched the flames leaping and dying in the fire.

'I didn't come away to fall in——' He stopped, then carried on. 'To fall for anyone, Sarah. I wasn't looking for——' His voice tailed away.

She finished the sentence for him. 'Action? A good time?' There was a twist in her voice that made him hold her tighter.

'Stop it. Don't insult yourself—or me.'

'I'm sorry, that's what it usually boils down to, out here. You only have to look around.'

'Usually doesn't mean always. You're too defensive by half.'

'I need to be,' she protested. 'You know what it's like.'

He turned her head with his hand, making her meet his eyes. 'Not with me, you don't need to,' he said and there was a seriousness in his tone that made her melt and quiver inside. 'I won't trick you or hurt you in any way, Sarah. And I certainly won't foist myself on you if don't want me to.'

She held his eyes until the tension between them was almost unbearable. Then, slowly, deliberately, he tipped her chin and found her lips, in a kiss that went on for ever, first warm and tender, then harder, more urgent, until he groaned and shifted to take her more fully in his arms.

Still his lips held hers, while his hand gently held her head and his tongue parted her mouth and probed the warm softness inside.

She was lost in the feelings he was arousing in her, the loosening spirals of sensation that were unwinding to the furthest points of her body, the hollow quivering in her stomach.

His hands stroked down her neck to the opening of her robe, and paused there. He drew his head back, his lips parted and a dark flush along his cheeks, and looked into her eyes; whatever he read there made him utter a small sound in his throat and reach for her again, while his hands moulded the lines of her shoulders and breasts beneath the thin cotton.

Now it was she who gasped and moved against him so he could find her warm skin more easily. An insistent throb of longing was starting up inside her, beating out its need for fulfilment. She moved her hands impatiently against his chest, finding the thin cotton of his shirt an unbearable irritation. When his fingers probed beneath the lace and silk of her camisole and found the soft curves and hardened tips of her breasts, she gasped against the feeling his hands aroused.

Somehow they had moved on the floor until they were half lying, length to length, with the flames of the dying fire lighting them in a flickering glow.

She could barely see his face now, it was all shadow and mystery as he drew back from her lips to kiss her nose and eyes and ears, then down to her throat and the swell of her breasts, but the feeling of his lips was warm and right, and the smell of his skin against her was the headiest perfume she had ever known.

And she felt safe in his arms, she realised, safer than she ever felt with anyone before. She trusted him totally and knew he would always warm her and protect her, and keep at bay her fears and uncertainties.

Always? One tiny part of her objective mind examined the word that had slipped along her thought-stream. Who had said anything about 'always'? Certainly not James, who had been careful to make no commitment beyond acknowledging that some 'thing' had grown up between them.

Tonight was tonight, and by the end of the week he would be gone. That was how it always was with skiing romances—in fact that, in her brief experience, was how it was with any sort of romance—and there was no reason to suppose their affair would be any different.

Her thoughts intruded unpleasantly. She moved

her position, aware too that one arm was getting cramped. James let her go at once.

'What is it?' he murmured.

She grinned grimly. 'Cramp.'

He smiled. 'It's hardly surprising. Here——' He got up and offered a hand. 'We'll sit decorously on the sofa and finish our drinks over some civilised conversation.'

She got up, too, hastily rearranging her robe. He had seemed almost glad to have an excuse to break their embrace, she thought, and that made her feel despairing. They sat side by side, and there suddenly seemed nothing to say.

'I didn't ask you, how was your meal?'

'I don't know. I couldn't eat it.' There was bitterness in her tone.

He took her hand, turning it in his, looking at the fingers as he spoke. 'Why not?'

'You know why.'

Her eyes flicked to his, challenging him with raw honesty. He met her gaze levelly, deeply.

'Yes,' he said slowly. 'At least, I can guess.'

'Well, you must have seen it often enough before—chalet girls falling for your charms.' Was that her voice? So hard and nasty? What was happening to her?

James leant forward and his voice, too, was hard. 'Sarah, stop that. Right now. You're not a "chalet girl" to me, you never have been.' His eyes scoured hers. 'You don't believe me, do you? Well, I'm telling you the truth. Right from the moment I first saw you. I knew you were different.

'At first I thought it was the way you looked, so beautiful and healthy and full of life. You positively glowed for me. But later it was all the other things about you—your spirit and patience and good humour, the way you dealt so tactfully with everyone here. There's a million other things. Shall I go on?'

She shook her head, her throat tight with his words.

'Well, I will. There's something else—your un-flinchingness, the way you look things squarely in the eye and don't allow yourself any illusions. But,' his voice harshened, 'that can be carried too far, you know. You can end up so busy looking for unpleasant truths that you fail to see all the good things right in front of you.'

She gazed at him doubtfully. There was real force-fulness in his tone, true anger. She guessed that was the way he had addressed himself, as he'd goaded himself back to life after his accident.

'I just feel all at sea. I don't know what's happening. I've never felt like this before, never. It frightens me.'

He was silent for a long moment and when he spoke his voice was low. 'I've never felt like this either, Sarah, and it frightens me as well. That's the honest truth. But do we have to find instant labels? Let's just enjoy being together, give it time, and see what happens.'

She nodded slowly. It made sense, except for one thing. There was no time. Only today and tomorrow and a few days after that. And, anyway, she knew already the word that her label spelled out.

James drained his drink and stood up. She stood up as well, and when he turned and opened his arms to her she went into them readily, hungrily.

This time it was different. He could feel her slight figure in its thin clothes pressed against him, and it roused him readily. She could feel it in the way he hardened against her, and in the growing urgency of his lips and hands.

He pushed aside her robe and cupped her breasts as he kissed her deeply and then more deeply still, and her hands went up to tangle in the thick dark hair of his head. Then his hands roamed her back, pulling him to her as if he could crush them both into one flesh. She yielded to him, arching herself to his body, unresisting to the explorations of his mouth.

When he led her downstairs to his room, she went readily, following the hammering needs of her body and ruthlessly crushing down the last niggling, doubting thoughts that threatened to spoil the moment.

He closed the door, leant against it and caught her to him again, kissing her and kissing her as if he could not get enough of the taste of her lips. His hands pulled the lace bow in her hair and loosened her hair around her face, then went impatiently to the belt of her robe, untied it and shrugged it away from her on to the floor. He slid his hands under the thin straps of her camisole and eased them down over her silky shoulders, kissing the hollows of her neck before lowering his lips to her warm, scented skin and arousing her to new heights as his mouth found her sensitive nipples.

She tore away his shirt and let her hands roam his powerful shoulders and feel the roughness of hair on his chest, kissing him wherever she could find him and tasting the salt of his skin.

His breath was coming in harsh rasps from his throat as he spoke against the hollow of her shoulder. 'Will you stay with me tonight?'

Her answer was to reach up and pull his head down closer to her.

'Are you sure? Really sure?'

'Yes. Oh, yes.'

She felt the drumming of desire in her body. She wanted it, she wanted it more than she had ever wanted anything in her life. It would be impossible to return alone to her solitary room. That, at least, she was sure of.

From that moment on, taking her at her word, James' thoughts were only for her. She felt his intensity, the driving concentration that made him what he was, centred on her and her alone, her eyes and lips and throat and shoulders, on the person she was and what she had come to mean to him.

As each kiss deepened she began to know the full power of him, the overwhelming certainty of purpose that would take him to the absolute limits of any path he chose to pursue.

Now his goal was to slake his hunger for her, and in doing so to take her with him to the highest point of their mutual passion. His lips were tender, then hard and harder still, punishing himself and her in his driving need to bring them closer than two human beings could possibly be.

Because it was James, it did not frighten her, but inflamed her until she was like a woman possessed. She did not care what she said or did, or what moans of pleasure came from her lips. She threw her head back and offered herself to him, free and wanton as her hips arched blatantly to his and he pulled her tighter to him.

He freed his lips and drew back to look at her, unsmiling as he took in her heightened colour and parted lips.

She was overwhelmed by the force of drumming need he roused in her, and she found herself moving against him, urging his lips back to hers, taking his hands to hold her still tighter against him.

They did. Very slowly and deliberately he slid his grasp down below the white line of lace at her hips, his palms flat against the small of her back, his fingers seeking the cleft of her buttocks.

'Oh, James. Oh!' They were barely words, more groans of exquisite pleasure. Now the drumming was faster, more urgent still. Hands that were not hers but those of some other woman, a woman mad with desire, tore at his belt to free him from unnecessary clothes.

His body was magnificent, lean and strong and every bit as aroused as her own.

'Oh, God, for goodness' sake, let's get to bed, Sarah!'

They stumbled together to fall heedlessly on the plumped white duvet, laughing, gasping and reaching instantly for each to her. Then they were kissing again, their bodies beginning to move together in the same instinctive harmony that they had known all day on the mountains as they winged down the snowy slopes.

She could bear it no longer. Every inch of her throbbed and ached for him and she rolled back, pulling him over to her, open and vulnerable to him.

For one moment he raised himself on his hands and looked deep into her eyes.

'Sarah?' he whispered, and waited for her reply, although she knew what it cost him to hold back at that moment.

'Yes.' Her voice was little more than a croak, but it did not matter, for the small sound she made was swamped by a sudden burst of noise outside in the hall.

The front door was flung open, there were shouts,

stamping feet, the noise of jackets being unzipped. Then there were other noises, smothered gasps and giggles and stumbling footsteps up the stairs outside the room.

The moment was ruined. She found she had instinctively tensed from the instrusive sounds so close at hand, and James sank back on to the bed at her side with a bitter groan.

The sounds came and went, too insistent to ignore, too elusive to identify easily.

After a time, though, the voices distinguished themselves. One was Ned's and the other Kerry's, and they were both obviously drunk so that their conversation was erratic and punctuated by long, languorous silences. Fianlly there was the sound of shutting doors, then nothing.

'Thank goodness.' James murmured and, propping himself on his elbow, lightly caressed her breast. It stiffened instantly beneath his touch and the beat of heat in her body started up again in response to his gentle fingers. His face in the darkened room was brooding and beautiful. She turned to reach for him again, and they kissed, moving together again with an absolute certainty of purpose, but with a luxurious slowness more sensual than the headlong passion of before.

Then, from Ned's room above them, slowly but more and more instrusively, came the unmistakable noise of rhythmically creaking bedsprings. The noise was raw and rude, brutally animal-like, and it froze her heart.

Ned and Kerry. And even while poor Tim was still lying in hospital. How could they?

But why should she be so shocked? People did it all the time. Every Janet and John. Every Peter and

Jane. And sometimes Janet and Peter and John and Jane. She'd seen it all, and more, during her time in the skiing business. But it was horrible, her mind cried, debasing to the human spirit.

She felt all desire seep away from her. James' hand on her thigh was just a heavy weight, his breath on her cheek was too warm, too close. She drew back.

She had thought it was different, her and James. It felt different. But it wasn't. It was just another quick fling, another Alpine frolic. To the outside ear their bedsprings would sound no different from the creaking of those directly above them.

They lay unmoving, petrified figures, and as they did so the bedspring chorus rose to a crescendo and subsided.

James flung himself away from her, back on to the bed.

'What is it?' he asked dully.

'I'm sorry,' she got out. She didn't have words to explain all that she felt.

'It's Ned, isn't it?'

'Yes.'

How could it be anything else but those ghastly noises off? Surely he could understand that. But she felt him retreat from her in his mind, growing colder, harsher.

Then he flung himself up and strode across the room for his clothes.

She watched as he dressed.

'Where are you going?'

'Out. Where do you think? For a walk.' He turned and scowled at her, his face the dark stranger's face that he had showed her in the first few days at the chalet. 'I'm far too frustrated to sleep—even if you did have the courtesy to go back to your own room and leave me in peace.'

'Oh!'

The bitterness in his voice stung her. It was far greater than any simple physical disappointment merited. It seemed as if he hated the sight of her.

She knelt up on the tumbled duvet, careless of her nakedness, her hands out as she willed him to understand.

'I'm sorry. I don't know what happened. It all just——'

He dashed a hand down, scything away her words.

'I'm not stupid, Sarah. I know perfectly well what happened. What I don't know—what I'll never be able to fathom in a month of Sundays—is just what you see in that wishy-washy brother of mine!'

Then the door closed and he went out.

CHAPTER TWELVE

IN THE first grey light of the early morning the resort looked unreal, like a film set. The runs were empty of flying figures, the ski-lifts were caged and unmoving. As she watched, the sun began to tint the snow a delicate pink and curls of smoke rose lazily from one or two chalet chimneys.

She blinked, her eyelids scratching with fatigue. All night she had turned restlessly on her bed, unable to sleep, until at last, as the grey square outside her window lightened, she had dressed, let herself quietly out and walked up the hill to a place where the track opened out to a panoramic view down into the valley below.

She had hoped her old friends the mountains would restore her peace of mind, but it was just the opposite. She felt removed from the scene below her, no longer part of it, no longer part of anything, not even a coherent whole, just pieces of fragmented thought and bitter memories flying apart in all directions.

It was all such a mess and a muddle, and the worst thing of all was that she did not know what to do to put it right.

James was convinced she was involved with Ned. Last night had been the final straw, when he had assumed her sudden coldness stemmed from a simple jealousy of Kerry. Up till then—despite the repeated evidence of his own eyes—she guessed he had been prepared to accept her constant denials that there was anything between them, but not any longer.

She should have stopped him from stalking out, tried to explain the difficult truth—but what could she possibly have said? That the brutal sounds of enthusiastic lovemaking upstairs had suddenly made her realise what they themselves were doing? He would have thought she was mad, especially after he had taken such care to make sure that she really did want him to take her to bed.

And she would never have been able to find the right words to explain the full complexities behind the abrupt freezing of her ardour. She had gone to bed with James because she loved him. It was as simple as that. She had known it from the first, and then known it fully and consciously last night, as she had allowed the precious word to take shape in her head.

But he did not love her. He had never even hinted of such affection, at most he had talked of 'this thing' between them. But he had also talked, quite clearly and explicitly, about his past and all the girls he had casually made use of. And what was it he had said, when they were up on the mountain together? Nothing lasts for ever. She knew no warning could have been clearer.

She sighed heavily and her breath puffed out in a frozen white cloud on the cold air.

Last night she had simply ached for him. All reason had been stripped away from her. All she had wanted was for him to make love to her and ease the terrible longings of her body, and because of that she had ruthlessly banished any doubts from her mind. But she had been wrong.

The way they had reached for each other, roused

each other, had been heady, but it had been little more than brute desire. She could see that so clearly now, in the cold grey light of day.

There had been no tenderness or restraint between them once the bedroom door had closed, only a desperate need to take the fulfilment they both craved.

Perhaps it would have come later, once their first urgent hunger had been eased? She hung on to that thought like a pathetic rag around her dignity. But she would never now know.

She sighed again, bitterly. It was so stupid that James should think she had any interest in Ned! She knew he found it an impossible, almost incredible thought, yet since he'd first arrived at the chalet events had constantly conspired to confirm his suspicions.

If only she could tell him the truth and lay the whole petty deception out in the open. It wouldn't make him love her, or dissolve the aching pain in her heart, but at least they could part without this ghastly misunderstanding between them.

But loyalty to Gail and Brian had to seal her lips. She knew nothing about the state of his negotiations, but it could not possibly help their case to have one of their key chalet girls reveal herself as a hopeless cook and a devious actress to boot. Any businessman in his right mind would surely begin to wonder what else was not quite right beneath the surface of the apparently smooth-running company.

But worse than all that would be having to reveal herself to James as a liar and a cheat—she could imagine only too clearly his contempt for her when he remembered how demurely she had accepted his and everyone else's lavish praise for Ned's delicious meals.

She flushed fiercely even thinking of it, but as the chill of the morning cooled her cheeks so she took hold of the thought and examined it more closely.

Of course, if she was honest, that was the real problem. It wasn't just a question of Brian and Gail, but of her own fierce pride. She wanted James to think the world of her, and never to know the depths of lies and petty deceit she was capable of.

But he already held her in contempt for what he saw as her inexplicable involvement with Ned. Surely anything was better than that?

Her hands in her pockets were gripped tight as she unravelled the layers of thought. Her face was pale and her eyes red-rimmed by tiredness and tears. Then she decided. She would go to him now, this very minute, and no sooner had she framed the thought than she was turning to head back down the track.

As she did so she heard metallic clankings in the valley below. She turned. The resort was coming to life. Slowly the ski-lifts began to turn, bright red cabins rising slowly up the mountainside on their day's ceaseless circuits. Inside them she could see a scattering of heads, and knew they would be early-morning workers heading out to open up the higher lifts, and the bars and restaurants scattered among the slopes.

It was a complicated business, keeping a ski resort running efficiently. Everything needed to work smoothly, from the smallest drag-lift to the most lavish mountaintop restaurant.

And it was no easy matter building a skiing company up from scratch either. Gail and Brian had worked night and day for five years to extend their business from its first cheap coach trips and basic hostels to the thriving business it was today. They would want to see a proper return for their efforts.

She scowled to herself at the complicated entanglements she was enmeshed in. If she now confessed her failings to James, who knew what the results might be . . . She chewed her lip so hard, she felt the salt taste of blood. But if she resigned first, distancing herself and her deceptions from the company . . . The thought came to her abruptly, but made immediate sense.

She looked at her watch. It was too early to phone London, but time she headed back to start preparing breakfast. She dreaded seeing James again, seeing his dark, contemptuous eyes go over her, and them both knowing the full awfulness of what had happened last night. But if he had any tact or delicacy he would surely keep out of her way this morning.

She set off down the hill, fearful and forlorn, but at least at peace with herself over what she had decided to do. But it was only Kerry who finally appeared for breakfast, not bothering to hide the fact it was Ned's room she sauntered out of.

'Have you got a cigarette? I'm right out.'

'I don't smoke.'

'Well, coffee, then. Black.'

'It's in the usual place—on the warmer.'

Kerry raised languid eyebrows at her unusually snappy tone.

'Got out of bed the wrong side, have we, Sarah?' She made her way slowly to the coffee. 'And we don't need to ask whose,' she added casually.

Sarah froze, a piece of toast in one hand, a laden butter-knife in the other. 'I don't know what you mean.'

Kerry rummaged on the shelf and found a half-full packet of cigarettes. 'Thank God for that.' She blew out smoke, looking at Sarah through eyes narrowed against its sting. 'Oh, come on. Spare me the wide-eyed innocent look. I mean let's face it. I'm hardly going to be shocked, am I?'

'How's Tim?' she said, pointedly.

Kerry ignored the question, idly following her own thread.

'Ned predicted it, you know. In fact, we had a fiver on it. He said it was a certainty. I said I didn't think you were the type—more fool me.'

Sarah felt the toast in her hand begin to tremble as the hateful voice drawled on. She put it down hastily and turned away, but she could not shut out the words.

'When we came back and saw your jackets in the hall, I said you were both tucked up safe in your own beds, but Ned looked into your room and what do you know—the cupboard was bare!'

A flush of anger and embarrassment overwhelmed her.

'He had no right. And I don't want to hear any more, Kerry! You shouldn't judge everyone by your own behaviour. Just because you choose to hop into bed with someone new the minute your boyfriend is laid up in hospital it doesn't mean everyone else carries on that way!'

'Well, Sarah, it's whatever turns you on, isn't it?' Kerry seemed maliciously amused by her distress. 'I'm sure James' skiing is quite something, his parallel turns must be quite knee-trembling in their precision!'

'Stop it! Stop it! You don't know anything about James and me! Not every relationship is the sort of sordid one-night stand you seem to specialise in!' Anger drove the words out of her mouth, fast and hard. She no longer cared that Kerry was a client and that her role should be one of tactful service.

'Oh!' Kerry rolled her eyes. 'I suppose the next thing you're going to tell me is that it's true love, or something ridiculous like that!' Her mouth twisted with amused sarcasm. 'That really would be a turn-up, wouldn't it—true love striking on a chalet party? That would have to be a first!'

Sarah turned away, tears pricking red-hot at her eyelids. Kerry's sneering words put her own pitiful emotions in their true perspective. Only someone as love-crazy as she was could even contemplate such an absurdity.

'I really don't want to discuss my private life,' she got out. 'I don't care what you do, Kerry, and I don't see that it's any of your business how I spend my free time!'

'I'd second that—so I'd be grateful if you'd spare me the kind of censorious look I got when I came out of Ned's room just now.'

'I simply felt sorry for Tim.'

'Well, save your sorrow. Tim and I have an agreement. We always have had.'

Sarah turned away, sickened, while Kerry's voice drove on. 'It's not that uncommon, you know. It's how adults behave. I dare say James——'

'James what?'

The cutting voice startled them both, James had

come swiftly and quietly up the stairs into the main room, and was now glowering at both of them.

Sarah shot a glance at him and could see immediately that he had slept as little as she had. His gaze went to hers, black and harsh, and then cut to Kerry.

'James what?' he repeated, insistent.

Kerry levered herself slowly away from the wall where she had been lounging, and began to walk towards Ned's room. 'Oh, nothing, nothing important.'

Sarah watched her and could see that, despite the apparently languid movements, she was frightened by James' steely figure.

'I guess you two have plenty to talk over—I'll take my coffee elsewhere.'

She understood that fear. Alone with James, as the door of Ned's bedroom closed shut, she felt almost numb with apprehension. Last time she had seen him he had been in a black rage, staring down at her naked figure on his bed. Now his eyes held only grey contempt.

'She seems to know plenty about us—couldn't you wait to try and rouse Ned's jealousy?'

'Don't be absurd!' Her words were firm, but her voice trembled. 'If you must know, Ned looked into my room last night and saw an empty bed.' The words were out before she had a chance to realise how they would seem to him. There was a telling silence which she could not bear.

'Would you like some coffee?'

'Spare me your chalet girl niceties.' His voice was like grit.

'I wasn't being nice. Oh, what do you expect me to say?'

Now the tears were threatening to flood and spill. She clenched her teeth and clutched her fists into tights balls of determination. The last thing in the world she wanted at this moment was for him to see her weak and broken.

He shrugged, as if nothing in the world she said could be of any interest to him. 'I only came up to tell you I'll be leaving today.'

'Today?'

'I've just been telephoning the hospital. All the air ambulance arrangements are in hand. Tim will be leaving at midday. Since everyone else here is more than capable of looking after themselves and since there is hardly likely to be much pleasure to be gained from staying the rest of the time . . . If anyone asks, you can tell them urgent business called me away.'

Her eyes flickered across his set face. She loved him so much, it was like a huge raw ball of aching misery inside. 'James, last night——'

His hand scythed through the air. 'Forget it, Sarah. Let's both forget it. It was a mistake.'

'Yes, yes, it was. A dreadful mistake,' she echoed feelingly, remembering the drumming desire that had removed from her all sense and reason.

It had been a mistake for her because, loving him like she did, there was no way such a raw physical encounter could reflect her true feelings. All it could do would be bring more misery and aching loss in its wake.

Oh, James, James . . . The words yearned emptily through her head.

She felt his eyes on hers, scrutinising her closely, as if to probe the meaning of her echoing words.

'I see,' he said heavily, and turned to go.

'James!' She ran after him to the stairs.

'Yes.'

'What you think about me, about Ned—you've got it all wrong.'

'So you keep saying. But you never put me right.'

'I——' She remembered Brian and Gail. 'I can't now. Later. Can I talk to you later?'

'You mean, when you've straightened out your story with him?'

'No, I mean when I've made a telephone call.'

His eyes were as cold as steel. 'What are you saying?'

She took a breath. 'There was something between us. It started the very first day, before anyone else arrived——' His eyes darkened still further, she had not thought it was possible. Nervously she began to gabble. 'I got in deeper than I ever meant to at first, and he kept taking advantage of the situation——' Everything she said made it sound worse and worse. She was digging her own grave. 'Please, James——' Her hands were out to him in supplication. 'Let me explain properly.'

His mouth was tense, and there were frown lines about his eyes.

'I've got a taxi booked for twelve. I'll be in my room until then.'

Behind her she heard the sounds of Brad and Barbara stirring in their room. Any moment they would emerge, cheerful and talkative, demanding breakfast.

'I'll make that call now,' she hissed, and began to clatter down the stairs to the hall where the telephone was.

By some miracle of fate she got through the first time, and even more miraculously Gail was in the office to take her call. She raised her eyes to the ceiling in grateful thanks. Perhaps the gods had at last decided to be kind to her.

Their conversation was brief and to the point. Gail was stunned, Sarah could tell, but the edge of the controlled hysteria in her voice silenced her boss's questions. Sarah promised to write an explanatory letter, and she seemed willing to leave it at that.

But Gail's last words were ominous. 'I just hope, Sarah,' she said pointedly, 'that this sudden decision doesn't mean you're about to do something foolish. I never thought you were the type to let your heart rule your head—and you ought to know you're turning your back on a very bright future with NewSki.'

She turned to James' door. Maybe she was, maybe she wasn't. She no longer seemed to know who she was, or quite what she was doing any more.

Her knock sounded hollow. 'It's me.'

'Come in.'

James was folding clothes into a case and did not look up.

'I heard all that,' he said. 'I wasn't eavesdropping, but you can hear every word anyone says on the phone in this room.' His voice was hard and impersonal.

'That was the call I had to make,' she said dully. She put her hands behind her back and leaned against the door, watching him. She felt sad and bereft, as if all the long path of her life had led only to a dead end.

'I don't understand. Why have you resigned?' He finally looked at her.

'You've made a bid for NewSki?' she countered. He nodded. She took a deep breath.

'That's why I'm here. You were right when you said I wasn't what I seemed. I'm not a chalet girl, I never have been. I work in the head office, as a kind of general manager.'

' "The boss",' he said slowly, remembering the girls in the bar.

'When Annabel fell ill so suddenly, Brian and Gail asked me to step in and fill the gap. They told me you were an important client, and I had to do everything to keep you happy.'

He frowned. 'Are you telling me that's why you—we——'

'No!' she gasped. 'No, no!' Her eyes entreated him. 'How could you think that——'

'I don't know what the hell to think, Sarah. Why couldn't you have told me all this before?'

'I couldn't. I felt I owed it to Brian and Gail to keep on pretending everything was as it seemed. Ned told me about your interest in the company that night we went to Les Halles, and I knew how desperate they were to clinch a sale. They've done me a lot of favours in the past, and they're good friends. I didn't want to betray them, or make NewSki look badly managed—which it isn't.'

'I hardly think putting a senior manager in to cover for a sick chalet girl constitutes bad management. Rather the opposite.' He was looking at her closely, as if working to adjust his image of her.

'It is if she can hardly boil an egg,' she said bitterly. 'Chalet girls have to be able to cook.'

'Your meals have been excellent.'

'Ned's meals.'

'Ned's?'

'That's where Ned came in. He arrived to find me making a complete mess of cooking supper, and volunteered to step into the breach. It's his meals that you've been praising so lavishly all this time. Either he's done the cooking, or he's left me such meticulous instructions that even I couldn't go wrong.'

'No doubt expecting a few favours in return,' James cut in. 'That's my Ned. He never does anything out of the generosity of his own heart.'

'He said he wouldn't—expect anything in return—and I was desperate enough to want to believe him. But of course he did. And when I wouldn't comply he threatened to tell everyone about my incompetence. If he hadn't had his attention diverted by Kerry, I think it might have come to that——'

James was staring at her, a sweater held forgotten in his hand.

'I hated deceiving you like that,' she burst out, 'but I didn't want to let Brian and Gail down by showing up NewSki's feet of clay. They were crazy to think I could cope! Almost anyone would have done it better!'

She waited. The worst was over and the confession lightened her heart, but her eyes were locked to James' as she waited tensely for his reaction.

It came slowly. Gradually his face softened, smile lines deepening about his eyes which warmed from grey to blue. His mouth curved into an enchanting grin. He crossed the room and gripped her by her forearms.

'Nonsense,' he said. 'You absolute idiot, Sarah. Don't you know you've done a magnificent job? Forget the cooking, anyone can do that with a bit of training. But how many people have your tact and diplomacy? How many could have held Barbara's hand to ski school, then pushed her off on her own with such an energetic shove that she was forced to find her own feet? How many could have tolerated all Kerry's poisoned darts without losing their temper, not to mention Ned's drunken advances?'

'Oh, any chalet girl worth her salt could have coped with those——'

He ignored her. 'And what about Tim's accident? You gave up your free time, kept your head, interpreted what everyone said. Just think what it would have been like without all that.'

Her eyes were on him, wide. She had not known he had noticed all those things, let alone appreciated their worth.

'You mean you're not furious with me?' she got out.

He threw back his head and laughed. 'Of course not! Why should I be? I'm just so relieved that that's all your guilty secret amounts to, to know you aren't harbouring a secret passion for Ned.'

'I suppose I got it all out of proportion. I kept thinking about how you praised the cheese soufflé, and I simply sat there silently looking at you.'

'I probably only said it to see that wonderful smile of yours. All I wanted to do when we sat down for dinner was to gaze and gaze at you. When you talked, laughed, you seemed to light up the whole room.'

'You were so silent all the time! I was sure I'd displeased you in some way.'

'Displeased? Never. I was fighting the urge to reach out to you all the time—touch your hair, your lips, your perfect skin——'

Now his eyes were warm on her and his fingers stroked her hair and cheek. She searched the dark depths of his gaze, amazed at the intensity she read there. She felt light and free and suffused with love for him. When he gently raised her chin so that his lips could find hers, she yielded up to him like an opening flower.

It was so right, so perfect, so good to feel his arms going around her again and to be kissed by him, so gently and yearningly.

But quickly, too quickly, things changed again. Their bodies were still charged with all last night's longing, and his kiss soon hardened as he pulled her closer and moulded her body to his.

'Sarah,' he said, like a groan of distress, 'I want you so much.'

His words made her tense back from him. Last night she had been blind with longing, drunk with her love for him, but the thin light of dawn had shown her her mistake.

She opened her eyes and looked past him to the bed where his suitcase lay half packed, and her spirits plummeted from the heights to which he had raised them.

If she went to bed with him now, her loss would only be all the greater when he flew away.

'What is it? What's the matter?'

She was silent, dumb with misery.

'Sarah.' He drew her gently to the bed and made her sit beside him. 'What is it? You must tell me.'

She studied the carpet at their feet. He took her hand, but she could not look at him.

'Last night?' he prompted slowly, and a catch of apprehension in his voice made her raise her eyes to his. She saw a pulse in the muscle of his jaw and saw bruised hurt in his eyes. 'It wasn't Ned, then? I was wrong about that.'

'Not in the way you think.' The words came reluctantly.

'In what way, then?' he prompted.

'This is difficult—hearing Ned and Kerry together—it seemed sordid, somehow, so casual——'

'And you thought to yourself, "That's what I'm doing, and it's just as sordid and casual"?' Now his eyes did not leave her face. She turned to look at him squarely, finding courage.

'Yes. Yes, that's what I thought. I'm sorry, James, I should never have let things get so far.'

'It wasn't for me,' he said quietly, his hand tightened around hers. 'It most certainly wasn't casual for me.'

'What do you mean?'

He crooked his mouth. 'If things had not been so rudely interrupted, you would have found out. My head was full of plans. But perhaps I'd got it the wrong way round.'

'I don't understand.'

'I was so unsure of you. There was something elusive about you. No matter how close we seemed to get, you seemed always to be drawing back from me, hiding your real self. I knew how badly you'd been hurt, how hard you found it to trust anyone again, and I didn't know how to break through those barriers except by making love to you——'

'You—unsure?'

'Yes. Not about most things, but about you. I knew you would only let me take you to bed if you——' he paused '—cared for me. I thought that afterwards we could talk more honestly. There were all sort of things I wanted to ask you.' He smiled at her suddenly, with a look that lit his face with humour. 'Not least if you would help manage my new company—NewSki.'

'What?' The bombshell made her head whirl. 'You mean you've already bought it?'

He nodded, amused at her utter amazement. 'I'm afraid all your soul-searching was rather in vain. The deal was finalised three days ago. I wasn't sure who I would find to run it, but after a few days here the answer was perfectly plain. I'm afraid in my arrogance I thought I was spotting new talent, but now it's blindingly obvious to me that that sort of responsibility has been second nature to you for a long time.'

'I'm still flattered——'

'But that was only a conditional offer,' he interrupted her firmly. 'Conditional on the acceptance of my other proposal.' He paused and ran his hand softly, arousingly, up her arm. She shivered deeply. For a moment he seemed lost for words, and when he spoke his voice was low and husky. 'A real proposal, Sarah. I was going to ask you to marry me.'

'Oh.' The sound was little more than a catch of shock in her throat. She looked, open-eyed, open-mouthed, as the words sank home.

'Marry?'

'Yes, marry. To have and to hold—from this day forth——' He smiled at her disbelief, but there was apprehension in his eyes. She saw him swallow nervously, and her love for him overwhelmed her.

'I thought——'

'I know exactly what you thought. You thought it was just another ski-slope romance, over as soon as it had started. You thought I wanted to get you into bed, and then fly away without a backward glance in your direction.'

'Can you blame me? That's how things usually are.'

'I know. I've been there.' He pulled a face. 'But not any more, not ever again. Not since I've met you, Sarah. I've always known exactly what I wanted, and I want you and no one else, ever again. That's if you'll have me . . .' His eyes went over her, and she read their uncertainty and reached out to him.

'I can't believe you're asking me.'

'I think I fell in love with you when we were at the hospital together. You were so calm and capable— and yet you looked so absurd and fragile in that enormous nurse's overall I found for you. I love the contrasts in you, Sarah, all that strength and vulnerability mixed up together.'

'I think I knew when we first skied together.' She smiled at him, suddenly shy. 'I always fancied you, you must have seen that. But at first I thought you were so cold and withdrawn. I never thought we could have anything in common.'

'You mean——'

'I love you, James.'

'And you'll marry me?'

'Today, if I could!'

He smiled at the look on her face, so deeply and warmly that she thought it impossible she could ever have thought him cold.

'Unfortunately that's not possible. There's the little matter of us being in wrong country.'

Even as he spoke he was lifting her face, turning it to his so he could lower his lips on hers in an exquisite kiss of love. After a long, long time he raised his head.

'Oh, Sarah, my love.' His breath was uneven. 'I want to make love to you so badly, but I'll wait if you want me to, wait till you're my wife.'

In answer, she drew him to her. This time their kiss was another world. From somewhere, far off and unimportant, there was a clatter as his suitcase slipped from the bed.

'You might have that much self-discipline,' she said hungrily as she pulled him down with her on to the pillows, 'but I certainly don't.'

ℋarlequin American Romance®

Gull Cottage

The sun, the surf, the sand...

One relaxing month by the sea was all Zoe,
Diana and Gracie ever expected from their
four-week stay at Gull Cottage, the luxurious
East Hampton mansion. They never thought
that what they found at the beach would
change their lives forever.

Join Zoe, Diana and Gracie for the summer of
their lives. Don't miss the GULL COTTAGE
trilogy in Harlequin American Romance: #301
CHARMED CIRCLE by Robin Francis (July
1989); #305 MOTHER KNOWS BEST by
Barbara Bretton (August 1989); and #309
SAVING GRACE by Anne McAllister
(September 1989).

GULL COTTAGE—because one month can be
the start of forever...

ANNOUNCING . . .

The Lost Moon Flower
by Bethany Campbell

Look for it this August
wherever Harlequins are sold

HR 3000-1

From the *New York Times* bestselling author Patricia Matthews, the saga of a woman whose passion for gems leads her to fortune . . . and love.

Sapphire

Patricia Matthews

A strong-willed woman with a dream of ruling her own jewelry empire travels from London to the exotic India of the early 1900s in search of rare gems. Escorted by a handsome rogue, she discovers danger, paradise, riches and passion.

Available in September at your favorite retail outlet, or reserve your copy for August shipping by sending your name, address, zip or postal code along with a check or money order for $5.25 (includes 75¢ for postage and handling) payable to Worldwide Library Books:

In the U.S.	In Canada
Worldwide Library Books	Worldwide Library Books
901 Fuhrmann Blvd.	P.O. Box 609
Box 1325	Fort Erie, Ontario
Buffalo, NY 14269-1325	L2A 5X3

Please specify book title with your order.

SAP-1

 WORLDWIDE LIBRARY

Harlequin Regency Romance™

Romance the way it was *always* meant to be!

The time is 1811, when a Regent Prince rules the empire. The place is London, the glittering capital where rakish dukes and dazzling debutantes scheme and flirt in a dangerously exciting game. Where marriage is the passport to wealth and power, yet every girl hopes secretly for love....

Welcome to Harlequin Regency Romance where reading is an adventure and romance is *not* just a thing of the past! Two delightful books a month.

Available wherever Harlequin Books are sold.